ALICIA'S MISADVENTURES IN COMPUTER LAND

Magic Prose Publishing
publisher@magicprose.com

ISBN: 1-5029-1390-9
ISBN-13: 9781502913906
Library of Congress Control Number: 2014919248

Belinda Vasquez Garcia

Some Illustrations by Jessica Dunlap

Composite Illustrations by Belinda Vasquez Garcia

http://magicprose.com/chaos-computing

Contents

1. Computer-gnomes Ate My Homework

"Computer-gnomes ate my homework," I shouted.

The science teacher and principal at Genius Middle School hung their mouths open like clueless dinosaurs.

"Surely, two smart men like you have heard of appliance-gnomes?" I said.

"We have no such knowledge of this new technology, Miss Alicia," the balding men recited.

"Appliance-gnomes steal socks from clothes dryers." Each man wore 1960 sandals. The principal had a red sock and brown sock. The science teacher wore a blue sock and yellow sock.

They both yelled, "So that is what happens when the dryer stops spinning. Gnomes steal our socks! Thank you for enlightening us, Miss Alicia."

I then explained that computer-gnomes are high-tech cousins of appliance gnomes. Computer-gnomes buzz inside computers gobbling book endings and swallowing song notes. Gnomes slap advertising across interesting gossip.

"Well, well, so it's gnomes who pop up those ads!" The principal rubbed his hands together. Our school leader will announce this revelation tomorrow morning over the school loudspeaker.

"Place your ear against the computer and you might hear tiny hammering or singing," I ordered.

The science teacher crawled under the principal's desk, ripping his coffee-stained pants.

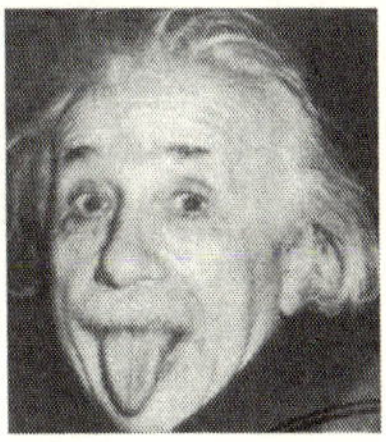

Are those coffee spots? His *Albert Einstein* undershorts showed through the tear. The *God of Science* stuck his tongue out from the crack.

The science teacher shoved his ear against the PC tower case. "Miss Alicia is 100% correct! I can hear gnomes singing." The science teacher hummed along, sounding a lot like a fan.

"Homework is the main diet of computer-gnomes," I added.

The science teacher and principal looked dumbfounded.

"Homework is full of fiber," I pointed out.

Now everyone knows old people eat a lot of fiber so they can fart a lot. The teacher and principal both finally understood that, "Computer-gnomes ate your homework. Computer-gnomes must be well educated and healthy. You are dismissed, Miss Alicia." Fart. Fart.

I swaggered out of the principal's office, waving my hand across my nose.

Computer-gnomes ate my homework! I slid down the wall, hugging my stomach and laughing. I am President of the Chaos Computing Club and would never have any problems involving computers. I am a first-class computer hacker born able to type 300 words a minute. My mouse is vertical and roars like a gaming joystick. My keyboard can be shaped like a tent. These two ergonomic pieces of hardware allow hacking into computer websites, email, etc. for hours. There is no worry about aching wrists while scanning a neighbor's bank account.

I swear to the computer gods that I am no thief! My 14 year-old brother Axel is.

The funny thing is though; lying about the past sometimes predicts the future. Some might call this karma—be careful what you lie about, because it may come true. I believed I knew everything about computers until one evening; computer-gnomes swept me away.

So grab a soda and a slice of pizza. Get comfortable to hear a story that I swear on all my hacking awards is true—computer-gnomes really do exist! You see, it was a dark stormy night and...

2. I Find Out About Gnome Repellent

Have I crowed about being a night owl? Most hackers are. A hacker's natural aptitude is spying. I flattened my body against the wall, blending in with blue wallpaper in our hallway. The fabric of my ballet dress has stars for night espionage.

It was midnight, the time of day when computer pirates sail the high seas of the World Wide Web!

A pirate was looting those same seas in the family study.

The keyboard clicking stopped.

Chair wheels squealed across the study floor.

Footsteps pounded down the hallway towards the bathroom.

I slid from the shadows and danced lightly on ballet slippers, twirling on my piggies. Alas, my toes are more like hooves causing me to stumble through the study doorway like a cow.

I snapped the lock in place. "Ha! Gotcha, Axel! My computer now."

Axel is a gamer and pirate so our battle over computer use is ongoing. My brother usually wins our fights, but it was Friday the 13th, my lucky day! My hacking magic works best during a full moon because I am a techno witch.

Whistling, I hung my ballet slippers across my neck and slipped my aching toes into sneakers.

I pointed the mouse at the letter *X* on the monitor screen, closing down Axel's computer game.

I swept an arm across the desk, toppling a score sheet and strategy papers onto the floor.

"Alicia, open up," Axel screamed, banging on the door.

I threw the DVD holder for *Screen Burn-In & Other Ghosts Game, Beta Version 1.0* at the door. "You've been on the computer all evening, so shut up, Axel! I have ended your session, preventing you from advancing to Master Player! You already have a fat head. *Oh, I'm such a master gamer,*" I mimicked his boasting.

"I'm going to find a screw driver to remove the door hinges," Axel shouted, rattling the handle.

"Ha! You suck with hardware, you sissy!"

I banged my fingers on the keyboard, logging off Axel's account and then logging into my user account.

A serious hacker stretches before a session. I was so good at cracking my knuckles and flexing my fingers that the noises played Justin Bieber's *Believe* album.

I had designed an animation from several pictures of myself to use as my user background theme. My image now danced across the monitor screen, kicking at soccer balls.

Thunder cracked against the study window.

"Smile," the computer speakers blasted. The digital camera mounted on top of the monitor flashed. Funny thing is I had not taken a selfie. A hacker who goes by the handle, Caterpillar, enjoys breaking into camera software. "I warned you to never take my picture, Caterpillar," I yelled.

The computer made a whiney sound, followed by an exploding noise and sparks.

The computer screen went black.

"Come on, dumb machine, work!"

A vital lesson about computers is to *never kick the hard case to start the machine as you would a broken toaster*. The hard case of a computer is called hardware for a reason.

I hopped on one foot and mimicked Dad's voice, croaking and sounding like a frog. "Do not touch my computer without permission, Alicia."

Ergonomic typing gloves make great fingerprint wipes.

The lightning ended, making it safe to poke a pen against the power button. A pen does not leave fingerprints. Technically, I was not touching Dad's computer. Besides, Axel and I spend more time on the computer than Dad does. My brother and I have squatter rights so the computer belongs to us.

The computer was still dead.

I jerked the power cord from the wall. To test the outlet, I plugged a radio in.

A radio announcer cackled, "Oh dear! Oh dear! I shall be too late!"

A sound like tiny footsteps ran under the study sofa bed. *Mice?*

Under the sofa bed was only the camera lens and stale popcorn. I pushed the lens back into the computer camera and munched on a few kernels.

"Oh my ears and beard, how late it is getting!" blasted from the radio.

I unplugged the radio, shoving the computer plug back into the outlet. There was still no green power light.

Now here is the raw deal. My parents actually believe that their two children will not spend so much time using the computer if the monitor is one of those bloated kind that looks like a television set from the caveman era.

As if the old monitor was a looking glass, my face stared back wistfully, revealing a freckled girl with mousy-brown hair hanging in strings to her shoulders. My reflection showed a hacker all dressed up like a ballerina. The storm ruined my evening plans of browsing the web and watching a ballet in Manhattan or even Russia. Who cares if the performance is years old!

I yanked my ballet slippers from my neck, throwing them in the air with disgust.

Aha! The computer has a keyhole with an arrow pointing to the word *locked* engraved on the case. The machine must have turned to the *locked* position when lightning struck, turning itself off, perhaps as a safety precaution.

I ransacked the desk drawer for the computer key, but only found a lipstick tube, which I stuffed in my waistband. A girl never knows when she might run into Justin Bieber, which is why I sometimes comb my hair. A pop star like Bieber would require clean teeth and minty breath. I sprayed my fingers with Peppermint Monitor Cleaner and then rubbed my digits across my teeth.

Ah, there is gold beneath the desktop, chewing gum that is. The gum sort of like my spit. Axel has a big mouth, like all boys, so this wad might be his.

I blew the bubblegum like a puffer fish.

The bubble popped at the same instance a thunderbolt exploded.

Sticky gum plastered my computer eyeglasses that normally let me hack through the web like Superman with x-ray vision. Hackers talk to themselves since we spend loads of time by ourselves. "It's not my fault storms make me jumpy," I said.

"Not your fault?" echoed in the study.

Yipes! No one else was in the room.

"What's your login, eh, poodle?" the voice screeched.

The radio plug dangled from the desk, proving a radio announcer could not be talking.

Speakers hanging from the monitor could transmit a voice when the computer was on. However, the computer could not be working in the *locked* position.

The computer case is breathing! A ticking noise sounded like a heart.

The speakers squeaked, "Oh, dear, I'm going to be late."

"Caterpillar, is that you?" I whispered to my wise hacker friend.

"Login!" bounced off the study walls.

"You're freaking me out, Caterpillar," I screeched.

"I am talking to you, human, with white rabbit teeth, braces, and pimple on your nose. Log-in!"

I slammed a hand over my nose. The computer's power light was red, indicating the machine was off. Then why was it giving advice on curing acne? "The spots on my face are freckles, you moron! Freckles!"

The machine said, "People who have freckles are often in denial. They..."

I yanked the computer's power cord from the wall.

My heart creaked and folded like a wallet, as the keyhole on the machine turned by itself from the *locked* to *unlocked* position.

Caterpillar is a first-class hacker, worming his way through network connections. Even he cannot make the power light flash green on a computer with no juice.

"Skinny ninny!" hollered from the speakers.

"I am not skinny!" I shouted.

"Login! I need your name, you nincompoop!" the unplugged computer said.

Engraved in gold letters on a piece of shiny metal on the box that held the guts of the computer was the name, *Enchanter*. Now, I, of all people know that a computer is not magic. Enchanter was the model name of the computer, yet I said in a breathless voice, "Enchanter, is that you?"

A stick horse materialized on the monitor screen. The horse wore a French beret cocked jauntily on its skull. A mustache curled up on each side of its face. The horse rolled around the screen on a golden wheel. "I am risking my job by talking back to a mere user," the horse said in a snotty French accent.

Run, my good sense inwardly screamed.

Sometimes it pays to be nosy. Curiosity is an important skill for a natural-born hacker so I remained seated.

The horse spun its head around its stick, as if to see if someone was spying. Quickly, it reshaped into a golden lock that resembled locks hanging from school lockers, except for a flattened horse face.

The lock bounced across the screen, spitting as it spoke. "I am Monsieur Barebones, Head of Computer Security. The computer is in lockdown mode." His keyhole moved like a mouth.

The lock slammed against the monitor, causing its horse face to fill the entire monitor. "You, girly, I know who you are," he said, knocking against the glass. "You are Alicia, Offspring Version Two, who likes to blame others."

"I told Dad it was gnomes who broke the computer last week," I said.

"Eek! You have heard about the beasties!" The lock sprayed itself with a can labeled, *Gnome Repellent.* "The computer runs smoothly one minute, the next second, the machine is crashing. Gnomes are wafflers. The beasties help me plug a security hole, while spraying hoses at the firewall to let the pirates in. The raiders steal music, video, and other treasure. They sell their booty on the black market, PirateTreasureBay."

"Yeah, I know. My brother is a computer pirate."

"The pirates share their booty with the beasties. The gnomes have their noses in every computer chest."

"I made up computer-gnomes!"

"Shush, Alicia, do not anger the gnomes. Instead, take teeny-tiny baseball hats, boots, and blue jeans. Stuff the clothes in the DVD drive, one at a time, mind you. Include ashes from your dad's pipe. A gnome loves used tobacco, as you do, Alicia. I watched you pick up your dad's pipe and smell it. Ah, you can't get closer to your dad by sniffing his cold ashes."

"How do you know so much about me?" I said in a small voice.

"First thing your dad did when he set up this computer, was to load the hard drive with family files and pictures."

"Be quiet." Axel was outside the door, rummaging with some tools. "Where are the family files?" I whispered.

He was about to answer and then a humming came from the computer—a mishmash of voices blended into noise. Behind Barebones were padlocked iron gates guarding a dark and murky dungeon. Gawking eyes floated in the darkness.

Barebones beckoned with his wide nostrils. "Come closer, Alicia."

His voice was sinister sounding, but I have always been a sucker for a handsome stick horse. The stud's mane stuck straight up from his horsey head with hair gel.

I flattened my ear against the monitor.

Barebones whispered, "The beasties who infest this computer insist I unlock the gates and let them at you."

"Gnomes do not exist except as statues in gardens!" I insisted.

"The gnomes are curious about you. Do not worry, pretty girl. Barebones was programmed by gentlemen and will protect you from the beasties by not letting you login."

"Gnomes are nosy? Well, I am curiouser and curiouser. You are keeping me from surfing the Internet. So, scram, dog-food head!"

"There is no reason for insults, pimple face! Do not make me crosser than a French croissant. It is your own fault you cannot use this computer. Your dad downloaded me for free from shareware, just to keep you out, Alicia."

A familiar ache sank low in my stomach. *I am not a freak! I am not!*

"I read the documents your dad has on you in a file labeled, *Irresponsible Alicia*," he sang. Barebones stuck his tongue out. Well, maybe not a tongue, more like a wire piece fashioned to pick a lock.

Barebones turned back into a stick horse cloaked in a trench coat and Sherlock Holmes hat. His clothes had online-store sales tags. The horse peered through a magnifying glass, his eye covering most of the screen. "As Manager of Security, downloaded from the French Internet for free, I am programmed mainly with spyware. You show potential in your funny-looking photos. You are aged twelve years, like stinky cheese. Give yourself a chance, puppy; you may yet shine. Next time you throw your ballet shoes in the air, dance with them in the clouds. You are a soufflé, still rising. One day, you may be famous and a Quiche Alicia named after you, voila!"

"I am famous!" I said. I placed my ballet shoes back around my neck.

"No one has heard of you. Alicia is a girl with but one Facebook friend," he said.

I shifted my eyes to a red picture frame on my bookcase shelf in the study. The hacker Caterpillar was not only a friend but also my hero. The Caterpillar is a legend among hackers. We occasionally take online vacations together. His avatar is a smoking caterpillar. My avatar is a white rabbit.

I was about to reveal my secret identity when the stick horse goaded me about the file again.

"I want to read that file!" I pounded the chair-arms and hunched my back, spreading my fingers. I attacked the keyboard, slamming my fingers on the keys.

I turned the keyboard upside down, holding it in the air and typing.

I spun the keyboard back around, playing it like piano keys, from right to left, up and down.

Meanwhile, a screwdriver jiggled the door handle, followed by cursing.

Okay, so I confess. I am an expert at breaking and entering, just as Axel is. I closed my eyes, blindly clicking at the keys, laughing at my expertise. I clobbered the keys, stopping now and then to wipe my runny nose on my arm.

"Halt!" Barebones bounced across the monitor from corner to corner. "Oh, leave the keyboard alone, you...you cracker."

"Crackers are thieves, whereas I hack. Hackers are not malicious or destructive." I lifted my chin proudly. "On the web, I go by the handle White-Rabbit."

"Eek! The White-Rabbit!" Barebones sprayed himself with a can of *Cracker-Off*! "You are famous for breaking into the *Teen Choice Awards* and having your avatar hop across the television screen."

I laughed. "Yeah, the *Teen Choice Awards* was one of my better hacks. My avatar, White-Rabbit, looked so funny standing on the stage munching a carrot. Everyone believed the animation was part of the show until they read the words: **You have been hacked by White-Rabbit**. In the computer world, White-Rabbit represents me. Hacking into the computer network of the *Teen Choice Awards* was the only way an ordinary girl like me could attend."

"You are not ordinary. You experience life indirectly through your avatar!" Barebones aimed the *Cracker-Off* can and pushed the sprayer. It was turning out to be a weird Friday the 13th. *Cracker-Off* was packaged in such a strong cyber-aerosol can that the liquid shot through the monitor screen, soaking my forehead.

The repellent did not even slow my fingers down.

"I insist you desist and resist cracking the secret password," Barebones shouted.

A thunderous, lightning crack caused the monitor to flicker.

Even Mother Nature could not stop me.

"So electrocute me for hacking," I yelled.

"I just might do that," Axel screamed from behind the door.

A mighty thunderbolt shattered the study window. Glass flew everywhere. I covered my head, screaming.

Light flashes streaked across the screen.

"Duh, restart computer. Reboot. Restart computer. Reboot. Re...," Barebones stammered.

Whoosh!

Barebones vanished from the monitor screen.

The locked gates, which had been at his back, burst open. Gnomes ran out. The gnomes wore caps over their long hair and shoes too big for their feet. Some gnomes seemed to just be wearing grandfatherly beards.

The gnomes glared from beneath bushy brows.

The gnomes kept charging the monitor screen and flattening against the glass.

Axel pounded the door with his fists, yelling, "open up, Alicia!"

I smirked at the monitor, giving the gnomes a smug, come-and-get-me look. Of course, the gnomes were only avatars created by a computer programmer. My own avatar, when I hack and dig holes in network connections, is a white rabbit. The gnomes could not really *get at me* as Barebones claimed they wanted to.

A grunting noise came from the camera mounted on the left of the monitor.

The camera lens popped out, smacking my forehead.

One by one, gnomes jumped from the camera hole. With each camera flash, a gnome shot from the lens and into the study.

I swatted at the gnomes with printer paper. Here is the thing you need to know about gnomes—the tiny creatures are fast.

Gnomes climbed in my nose.

"Don't do dat," I said, sounding like a stuffy cold.

I sneezed. Gnomes flew out my nostrils, smashing against the monitor.

My advice is if you see gnomes coming, RUN!

Gnomes grabbed paperclips and snapped them open, stabbing my fingers.

Three gnomes carried a ballpoint pen and charged my stomach.

"Ouch!"

Other gnomes held up the stapler, firing staples like cannon balls.

Gnomes pinched my ankles, growling and biting.

Giggling Gnomes slid down my nose.

Others bounced on my eyelids.

"Stop it!" I yelled.

Here are critical facts about computer-gnomes. First, the cute little people really are beasts—a couple of gnomes were trying to saw off my hand with the letter opener. (Give me a moment to scream bloody murder. There.) Secondly, the tiny creatures are sneaky. While other gnomes attacked with office supplies, stronger gnomes tied me with Velcro used to hold computer cables together. It turns out the mouse that ran under the couch was actually a gnome who untied the Velcro from the computer cables while Barebones and the storm distracted me. Caterpillar never messed with the camera. Gnomes took my picture for some creepy reason.

Gnomes climbed from my shoulders to my head, using my hair strands like ropes. The gnomes dug their dirty feet into my hair making my scalp itchy.

"Get Off," I mumbled since several of the little buggers hung from my lip.

Gnomes chomped at my ears.

Gnomes stomped on my face and yanked my eyelids down.

One gnome, who seemed to be in charge since he was the only one wearing a red sash, stood on top of the camera with his fists on his hips. "Say, sorry," the gnome said with a lisp.

"Sorry for what? I never did anything to you beasties! Axel, help," I shouted.

My brother was hammering the door hinges to remove them. Consequently, Axel could not hear anything but the banging door.

Another thing you should know about gnomes is they have big mouths but are not very loud due to their smoking. Computer-gnomes are always hoarse from smoking.

The gnome standing on the camera said, "Oh our ears and whiskers, we are late for tea." He jumped on the button, flashing a red light in my eyes. Click! A lightning bolt crashed through the broken window, causing the camera flash to splash the room.

Electric sparks tingled from my head to toes. My teeth rattled fiercely, my upper switching places with my lower.

My body was lifted into the air, spun, flipped, and then turned back around. I clenched the chair-arms and was still sitting, dangling in mid-air, with the seat far below. My head scraped the ceiling.

"Help me, Axel," I started to yell until a gnome smacked Velcro across my lips.

An elderly gnome with a big, pointy nose yelled some magic words, pointing his fingers at me.

Whoosh! I shrunk to a tiny girl and floated down towards the desk. Four gnomes held out a grey scrap of material used to clean the monitor. I bounced on the peppermint-smelling thing.

Before shrinking me, the gnomes had removed my shoestring. They now flung the shoestring over the monitor where another gnome attached it with tape.

The gnomes carried me up the shoestring to the camera mounted on the monitor. One by one, the gnomes jumped into the camera hole. The remaining gnomes tried to shove me down the hole. My legs dangled in the camera hole and I clenched the edge.

The door busted open. Axel stood there breathing heavily. His shaggy brown hair was in his eyes.

I struggled to yell for help, but Velcro covered my mouth. A gnome poked my fingers with a thumbtack until I let go. I vanished down the camera hole, swirling into a place filled with computer-gnomes.

3. I'm Stretched like a Licorice Stick

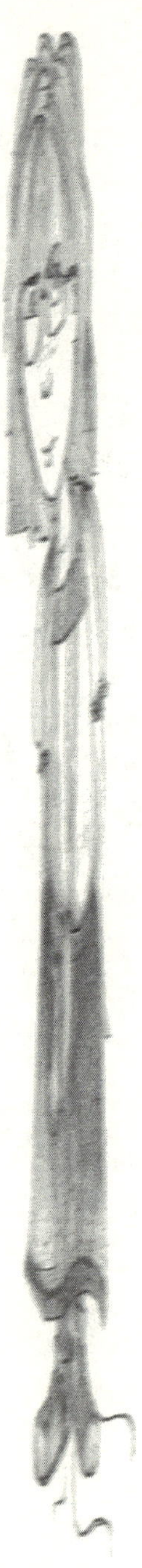

There was a loudspeaker announcement: "Attention all avatar shoppers! A pirate ship has just docked at memory Chip 342-2889-98881-05-5332-8788."

The gnomes snapped into smoke and vanished.

The noise of sparks, sizzling from wires dangling from the ceiling, caused me to nearly jump out of my skin. This place was dark and eerie. No horror film was ever this frightening! Where exactly was I?

The storm must have caused electrical burns to smudge a glass wall. In the waistband of my tights was a tissue. I rubbed a spy hole into the fuzzy glass wall and placed my blurry eye to the hole.

The keyboard was below. There were no gnomes jumping on the keys.

I rubbed with the tissue until the entire glass wall was clear.

Directly in front was the mirrored closet in the study. The mirror reflected a small girl standing in a frame. The girl must be my animated GIF that froze into a single picture when that awesome lightning bolt struck the study.

I flattened my nose against the glass wall, and the face grew bigger in the mirror across the room. The glass wall was like a magnifying glass.

I pulled at my hair and the image I thought frozen pulled at her hair. The rectangle that framed my face like a picture was the monitor frame. The gnomes trapped me inside the monitor—inside! This was the worst day ever in my entire life!

For no reason, my user account kicked in. My animated GIF image hurled towards me.

Holy tornado! I created the GIF from my photo, but now the GIF and I resembled clones, both the same size and flat.

Funny thing is, I never programmed my GIF with audio. She now sang, "I can't go back to yesterday because I was a different person then."

Soccer balls from my user wallpaper bombarded me.

My GIF lifted her leg at a ball, and missed, kicking my chin and causing me to stumble backward. "Who in the world am I? Ah, that's the great puzzle," she sang.

Ugh! I charged forward, slamming against the monitor screen. Ouch! That hurt! My panicked face was reflected in the study mirror. My tear-filled eyes looked wild with fear.

A gust of wind howled through the study window, which the storm had shattered. Axel carried a roll of wide duct tape and a stepping stool, along with a window-sized piece of plastic.

I ripped the Velcro from my mouth. "Help," I screamed with all the power of my lungs. My speech sounded funny since my teeth were upside down. In any case, we should have audio speakers embedded on the monitor instead of external speakers that plugged into the computer case. My voice was no louder than an ant.

My brother stood on the stool, taping the plastic where the window glass had been.

My tiny fists pounding against the monitor screen, but my tiny fists could not make the noise of a dropped pin. I yelled and cursed until my voice was hoarse.

Here is another rule of computers: Never let stress, tears, frustration, panic, fright, or fury cause you to fling your head at the monitor like at a soccer ball.

Ouch! An egg-shaped bump stuck out of my noggin.

"The gnome's magic changed me from a human girl to a virtual girl, but the pain in my chest is of a real heart, woven with blood veins, not electrical wires. My memory banks are intact, and I am still Alicia." My heart beat in my squashed chest. My mind functioned in my flat head, a place still filled with dreams. My tiny stomach growled with hunger. Real tears dripped down my cheeks. The tears tasted salty like a human girl.

My GIF image once more twirled by. My body was flattened and miniaturized but there was proof of my humankind. My animated image never changed its pattern, unlike me. I wiggled and jumped whenever I wanted and however my desire, because although I was now a virtual girl, I was a human virtual girl.

"Horrors, it is not logical for a human girl to be inside a computer monitor! How then is it logical to escape?"

"We're all mad here," my GIF image sang.

"Oh, shut up!" I threw a soccer ball at the GIF.

Eek! My important computer glasses, which sometimes doubled as a hairband, had vanished. "Boogers! The gnomes stole my glasses!" That is the second pair to vanish this year, "but the last time wasn't my fault either."

Wow! Inside a monitor, there is no need for eyeglasses. The study was as clear as rainwater. The now armless desk chair rocked, its springs creaking.

One chair-arm was on the study floor. I was holding the other chair-arm when the gnome shrunk me. I hugged the tiny chair-arm to my chest, rubbing my cheek against the leather. "There's no place like home."

There was a roar like a tornado, causing my background theme to crash. A rainbow replaced my wallpaper. Ruby-colored shoes fell at my feet. On closer examination, these were not ruby jewels but ruby computer circuits decorating fashionable wedge heels.

"Yippy! The computer God sent a gift!" I kicked off my sneakers and shoved my feet into the ruby shoes. The shoes were a bit tight.

I clicked the shoes together and rainbow-colored electrical sparks flew from the soles, along with a zapping sound. "There's no place like home. There's no place like home," I sang, closing my eyes.

The tapping of my shoes formed a rainbow.

The shoes laughed while fizzling to smoking, emerald-colored embers.

The ashes spelled out the words: You have been hacked by Oz!

I peeped out from the screen to the study mirror. Oh, my! The W-W-W hacked my computer. The W-W-W was head of the Oz hackers and went by the handle Wicked-Witch-West. The witch was actually a cracker, a thief, looking for gold at the end of the rainbow. She sent five Oz hackers to search the Internet for cracks. Do not let the little dog fool you. That avatar represents the smartest of these hackers working for the witch.

The hackers Dorothy and her friends were trying to figure out how to get over the rainbow. *Duh! Try walking under the rainbow, but tell the lion to duck his head. No wonder you owe money to the Wicked-Witch-West and have to work as her slaves.*

"I'll dig up your money some day, White-Rabbit," a voice cackled.

"I don't have a bank account, Witch," I yelled.

"I'll sell your human identity to the highest bidder, Alicia." Her wicked laughter faded.

I was busted! The witch knew who the White-Rabbit really was. Of course, I always hack using my avatar, White-Rabbit. I never should have bragged to Barebones about being the White-Rabbit. The witch will tell my enemies the White-Rabbit's real identity. She must think I am an animated GIF like my screen saver. No telling what will happen if she discovers my human form is actually stuck inside the hardware. "There must be a way out!" I thought with growing panic.

"I'm not sure what a monitor's guts are called, some sort of hardware, which is quite logical." I tapped my fingers against the rocklike monitor screen. "Oh, it's so hard to be stuck inside hardware." My head sounded hollow. "Hmm, I suppose humans are a mix of hardware and software. My brain is soft, but my skull is hard. My thoughts must be software, which explains my squishy brain."

Button rows lined the monitor screen. This first button looked promising until the monitor darkened. When pushed again, the monitor flooded with light. Good. The button is a toggle button, which is why pushing the button toggled between darken and lighten.

Another button shifted me to the right so that half of my body was visible in the monitor. Oops! "Shift back to the center of the screen."

The next button lengthened me so that my head pushed against the monitor ceiling. "Too tall," I screeched and reached out an arm stretching like licorice. Pushing the button made me shrink back.

The next button caused me to stretch sideways.

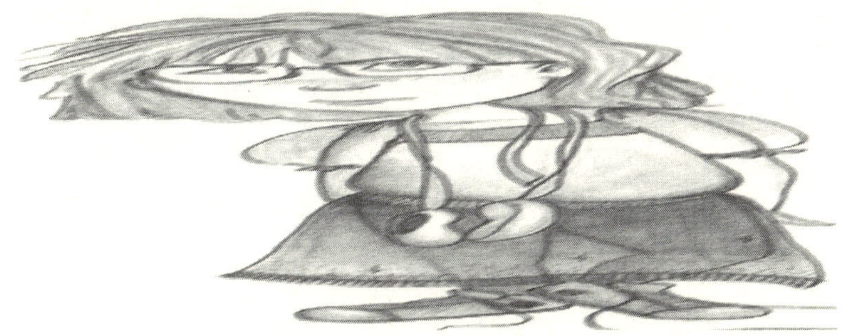

"Too fat," I yelled, pushing the button and shrinking back to my preferred size.

"Perhaps this other button." I rode down like in an elevator, sinking lower and lower. "Hurry, push the button before you vanish!"

I rose back up until all of me was visible.

Three more buttons to go.

"Maybe, the *Monochrome* button is an escape button, whatever monochrome is." This button made all color fade from the screen. "Too pale!" Pushing the *Monochrome* button again, painted the screen with color.

"This button reads, *Refresh*." The monitor light flickered and a giant hand grabbed my neck. The hand slammed me against the screen and then yanked back. The hand shook so hard that my teeth flipped back so the uppers were on top and the lower teeth on the bottom gums. The hand kept shaking.

"Please stop," I bleated, sounding like a goat.

The hand let go. Ouch! It then very gently placed a mirror on the floor before vanishing.

My hair was no longer puffed but combed in my favorite stringy fashion. "Refreshing!"

The last button read *Degauss*. An electric bolt shot at my wiggling body and lit me up with cobalt-blue lights. Magnets came out of the monitor wall. The magnetic force pulled at my fillings yanking at my braces.

"Ouch! Quit pulling my teeth out!"

At last, the bolt of electricity fizzled to a few sparks. The magnets retracted back into the monitor walls.

My hand was no longer wiggling so I could stuff my fingers in my mouth without poking my eye out. Thank goodness, all the teeth were there and the two fillings. The trouble was my parents were going to be angry because my braces were scattered on the monitor floor in metal pieces.

Hopefully, the monitor adjustments gained Axel's attention.

My doofus brother just walked out of the study, yawning. It was past midnight. Darn Axel! Why did he not wonder where his sister was?

Now that Axel was gone, earth was like a distant planet. The worst part—the degaussing folded me into a freakish staircase. My body waved about like an accordion playing a tearful tune.

Crying never helped anybody out of a frightening crisis, I thought. *Do not let fear get the best of you! Be brave else, you will never get out!* However, I was flat and now wrinkled like a folded piece of paper. My situation could not get any worse or so I thought!

4. A Bump on My Head Gives Me Advice

I examined my head in the hand mirror. The egg-shaped bump on my forehead had grown two eyes, a crooked nose, and a mouth.

I outlined my lips with the lipstick I found in the desk drawer.

The skin on my forehead stretched as the bump said, "We should go exploring."

"I must wait here for Axel," I said and gulped. The gnomes had come from a dungeon resembling a torture chamber.

"You might try using that lipstick to write for help to get us out of this pickle."

"You shouldn't compare our being stuck here to a pickle. My stomach is grumbling, and you resemble a hard-boiled egg," I said.

"Then you should try getting us out of this cucumber by writing with that lipstick."

"You'd make a tasty egg-salad, Eggy," I said.

The egg dictated in a hard-boiled voice, "Write: To Whom It May Concern—help! Computer-gnomes kidnapped us!"

I added to the message. *It is not my fault! I did not break the study window.* I signed the message, *Alicia* with a swirly *A*!

I colored Eggy's lips with the remaining lipstick.

"Now that you left a note, I relish us checking this place out," Eggy said.

"How would you like to be put in a ham sandwich instead? I'm the boss, so shut up already!"

"I'll clam up but if you scream, ice cream," Eggy said.

"Oh, be quiet about food!"

"You are irresponsible Alicia," Eggy sang, "and a boring chicken."

"Stop talking about chickens or I'll fry you! I am brave; else, I would not be here. However, this is a stupendous chance to go where no human has physically gone before and walk around inside a computer monitor with my own legs."

"I prefer to ride on your head. You hair smells strawberries." The bump kicked my forehead. Eggy had grown limbs.

"We will not go far. I am not irresponsible," I protested in a fading voice. I strolled with a big wide grin towards sparks sizzling from wires dancing above my head.

"A curious nature beheaded the Cheshire Cheese, and I'm sitting on your head," the bump whined.

"Keep your trap shut about cheese," I said, scowling. "Heads of cheese never wear fishing hats. That grinning head belongs to a cat fishing for the Wicked-Witch-West."

"Why doesn't the cat interrogate us then?" Eggy said.

"The cat is the witch's cyber familiar spirit."

The Familiar closed one eye, as if it was looking through a telescope.

"Scram, tuna breath," I said.

"Interesting," the cat hissed, "You are human."

Slowly, the Familiar's head faded.

"Please come back," I cried. "Don't tell the witch I'm human! Oh, Eggy, what am I going to do?"

"Hide," Eggy said.

We had no choice but to walk even further away from the monitor screen and into the unknown. It was both scary and exciting to think that there might be a secret world beyond the dark murky dungeon of computer security, besides gnomes and hackers.

5. I Meet a Mouse Named Louse

The monitor acted like a magnifying glass when I was closer to the screen. The further away, the more I shrank into an itsy-bitsy, virtual girl. The monitor ceiling was now high.

My accordion body bounced crookedly through electronic parts.

A sleeping, blue mouse hung by an extraordinarily long tail from a tree branch. His nose was shaped like a wheel. The tip of his tail was molded into an old-fashioned computer connector. Nailed to the tree was a sign with misspelled words that read, *Gided Computer tours by Louse-the-Mouse. Cheapest. Bestest Driving Tour this side of the Inturnet.*

Poking Louse in the eye did not waken him.

Curtsying caused my body to creak like stairs.

"My, aren't we the polite girl," Eggy said. "By the way, growing from your cabbage head gives me access to your memory banks."

"What are you implying?"

"You never curtsy; you yell. Your temper is like a hot tamale."

I punched the bump on its nose. "You're hurting both of us," Eggy said.

"Well, dummy up. We must make a good impression, and you're such a swellhead."

"That's because I come from you, smart aleck."

I cleared my throat. "We need a guide to take us out of this place please, Sir Louse."

The mouse snored.

"Wake up, cheese breath!" I shouted, flicking his nose wheel.

His nose spun furiously as the mouse swung around the tree branch, unwinding from his blue tail.

The mouse whizzed by too fast to grab him. He spun, until he unwound from the tree. The mouse flew straight down. He flipped open his eye which flashed red like an ambulance light.

"He's coming at us," Eggy screamed. The bump jumped off my head.

The mouse was bigger and landed with a thud, smashing me.

Eggy ran away yelling, "Where are the king's horses? Where are his men?"

"You bald-headed traitor, you may look like an egg but you're no Humpty Dumpty." I mumbled because my mouth was bashed into my lap.

The mouse landed on the black monitor floor with one ear folded back. His purple tongue hung from his mouth. His wire whiskers were bent out of shape. The mouse's breath smelled like lemon-scented furniture polish. His tail stuck straight up in a question mark.

"Whatever is wrong with you, mousey, is not my fault," I said.

"Program crash! Restart. Restart. One. Two...oh, Louse has the headache. Headache," he said. The mouse sat up, holding his head in his paws.

Have you ever noticed how a computer mouse likes to snack? Cookie crumbs were stuck on Louse-the-Mouse with dried cola.

The mouse made a grinding noise like an engine and gave two clicks with his tongue. He shook his rear end.

My head touched my lap, covering up my arms and hands, which prevented me from punching the mouse. Here is a warning about computers: never yell at a sleeping mouse.

Louse sniffed in a circle. "Well? What are you?" the mouse said.

"I can't explain myself I'm afraid, because I'm not myself, you see."

"Well, you're certainly not Louse, so you must be you," Louse said.

"You clobbered me," I said, sounding nasally. "Would you mind helping?"

The mouse wiggled me until my staircase-shape unfolded. I was still not my straight self but shaped like an accordion.

I pointed to the sign advertising tours. "You don't know how to spell."

"A mouse has no need for a spell checker. Is that what you are? A spell checker? Huh? Huh?" Louse moved one red eye closer. "You stink like sweat, sticky chocolate, bedpost gum, orange soda, and cheap roll-on deodorant. Aha, a thankless user!" Louse slapped himself on his cheek. His whisker wires wiggled with excitement. The mouse tried to lick my face.

"I do not stink and get your yucky tongue off me!"

"You are sticky with user stink," he said, yawning. The mouse rolled on his back, shivering. "I love users. Please, please touch Louse," he said, pushing his belly out.

The mouse was ticklish and purred like a cat.

"You didn't use the mouse clicker to sneak in, did you?" Louse said.

"I never clicked the mouse but used the keyboard."

"Ah, a cracker," the mouse said.

"I am not a cracker. Gnomes kidnapped me."

"Did the gnomes tell you where they hid their pirate treasure?" Louse shoved his eye in my face. "Huh?"

Louse was an optical type mouse and hypnotizing. "What treasure?" I said like a robot.

"The documents gnomes steal, such as the memory they rob, missing years from the calendar, movies, music, photos, icons, diaries, bank receipts, and various sundries. All their booty is given to pirates," he said.

"The Wicked-Witch-West may be involved, either in my capture or my escape. Her hackers are in the area. So is her Familiar."

The mouse screamed, "The W-W-W's cat is around! We must hide!"

"I offer you my protection in exchange for your guidance back home."

"Louse is guided by the user. You tell Louse how to get you back, and Louse will," he said.

"I'm a general user. I'm not a computer engineer!" I yanked at his nose.

He screeched, "Louse is an ergonomic mouse. Louse is designed to provide you comfort."

"First, something to eat then," I said, rubbing my empty belly.

"Hang on and follow Louse." He shook his tail in my face.

Louse tucked his chin into his chest and rolled like a ball. I skipped after him, holding onto his tail. His tail circled my arm. It was like skipping rope.

As mouses sometimes do, Louse got confused. He bounced in a corner, like a ball. "Oh dear, dear, Louse must find his center. Center," he stuttered.

Louse rolled faster, in bigger circles.

Louse's tail entangled my legs, dragging me along.

"You're making me dizzy," I yelled.

"There. There," Louse said, patting his own head.

"Quit repeating yourself before I bop you!"

Louse smacked his cheek. "Louse has his center back and is stable. Oh, dear, Louse's tail is tangled."

He rolled about, untangling his tail.

Once again, Louse tucked his chin into his chest and rolled like a ball.

I stumbled behind him.

Suddenly, a large eraser appeared and swiped at Louse.

"Help! I'm melting," the mouse screamed.

The eraser rubbed out his stomach, leaving a big hole.

I beat at the eraser with the chair-arm from the study.

The eraser wiped out a few of my hair strands, and I jumped out of the way, screaming.

It bounced on Louse's wheel and rubbed. The mouse's whiskers faded from view. Then his face vanished, followed by his body.

Finally, his tail disappeared.

All that was left of Louse were mouse droppings and a few black arrows pointing to where he had been.

So what if Louse was computer hardware? In this world of virtual beings, he was real. The mouse had guts, even if his intestines were wires. He had an intelligence of sorts, although he lacked memory. Louse had feelings and giggled when tickled. He said he loved users. "I won't cry, but oh, the same fate could still happen to me!" I sniffled and wiped my nose with my arm.

Without a mouse, I was lost!

"Lions and tigers and bears! Oh, my!" echoed from the monitor.

That dreaded giggling blasted from my computer speakers many times before.

"So you need a mouse? Well, here I am!" the squeaky voice hollered.

Louse-the-Mouse had been hacked and erased by an eight-year-old nightmare whose handle was Dormouse. The third-grader held a grudge for being kicked out of the Chaos Computing Club.

"Alicia, you pile of rabbit poo," he screeched.

Dormouse was aware of my human identity! My knees shook as his avatar slowly faded into view.

Dormouse pulled down his overalls, waving his fanny.

You ever been mooned by your computer mouse? That was probably Dormouse hacking in. The eight-year-old pervert gets his kicks taking control of computer mouses and popping up unsavory websites on computers. Dormouse was giving our hacking club a bad name, which is why we kicked him out.

"You're not showing me anything I haven't seen before, creep," I yelled at his furry mouse fanny.

6. A Dormouse Hijacks Me

Dormouse cussed up a storm. He threw cheese.

I caught a piece of cheddar. Thank goodness, since I was a virtual girl the food was real to my virtual stomach. I gobbled the cheese. "Thanks. I was hungry."

"Ugh!" he screamed. "You want your tea and eat cheese, too! I'm going to drown you in a teapot!"

A teapot suddenly appeared.

I ran around in circles, avoiding the pouring spout.

Dormouse chased me, shouting, "There's no place like home!" He peeled the chair-arm from my fingers and threw it on the monitor floor.

He grabbed my hair and yanked.

"Ouch! That hurts, you jerk!"

"You are feeling pain without wearing virtual reality gear? Where in the stinky cheese is your White-Rabbit getup? I ain't ever seen you looking like a paper doll before." He slapped his knee, laughing. "You got yourself in some fix, bunny! It is true like the Familiar reported. You are human!"

"You're working for the W-W-W now?" I said, feeling more scared by the millisecond.

"No one else would take me in after you squealed!" He kicked my shin. Dormouse growled at me hopping on one leg. "You cannot imagine what it is like being a dormouse working for a witch. She threatens to feed me every day to her cat. On top of that, the Familiar has it in for me ever since I poked the kitty's eye out. The witch knows my human identity. She threatens to tell my mother about my hacking. And it's your entire fault, Alicia!" Dormouse kicked my other leg and I fell at his shoes.

"You are in quite a dilemma. I could not have asked for a better revenge. That's what you get, White-Rabbit." Dormouse lifted his leg to step on me. "Ah, you're already flat."

It was typical for Dormouse to lay on his face pounding the floor in a temper tantrum.

"So you're hungry, huh?" he said, straightening his computer glasses and snapping at his suspenders, a sign the dormouse was temporarily sane. "Well, let's go to my mouse pad. I have a milk carton to show you."

Dormouse pushed and shoved me towards his hangout in the virtual world, which was a rubber shack. Tacked all over the walls were advertisement posters. There were ads for video games, comic strips, movies, clothing, cereal, and sports. The shack was a patchwork of magazine cutouts with no door, just a rusted keyhole.

He lifted a doormat, which read, *Not Welcome.* He picked up a brass key and shoved it into a keyhole. The keyhole squeaked open.

"I'm hungry," I said.

"Pick any stain you want and lick," he said, laughing.

There were soup, coffee, and mustard stains smeared all over his pad. Fingerprints were smudged on the walls. There was a jagged hole in a corner with teeth marks.

"You're a slob, just like my brother," I said.

"And you clean up your messes while hacking like a stupid girl."

Dormouse licked his whiskers, combing them with his paws. Shaking his rear, he walked to a table with crooked legs. A bread, cheese, and milk feast was laid out on top. There was but one plate.

Dormouse tied a napkin around my neck. He squeezed tightly.

"You're choking me," I said, coughing.

"There is only one napkin," he said, glaring. He bent his chin to his chest and pointed to the back of his neck.

I untied the napkin from around my neck and wrapped the napkin around his neck. "I don't need a napkin to eat any way. I don't make a mess," I muttered.

"Yeah, well you are in a mess." Dormouse poked the cheese loaf with a fork and a knife. He piled the slices on the plate. "You wouldn't like this cheese," he said, poking a chunk into his mouth. He chewed a mouthful while speaking. "This cheddar is avatar cheese, not human cheese."

Dormouse's eight-year-old human creator sat at his computer speaking through a microphone. If I was sitting at my computer controlling my avatar, White-Rabbit, I could take the food from him. It was awkward being a human paper doll inside a cyber world.

Dormouse lifted a milk carton to his lips, slurping the cream with his tongue.

The picture on the carton was of me! The gnomes had snapped my picture in the study. The gnomes then used the photo to let everyone know my human identity. On the milk carton, were the words: *Have you seen this hacker? The White-Rabbit, aka Alicia, is on our most wanted list.* The ad then quoted my email address.

My body waved back and forth like an accordion. "Ah, music with Dory's meal. You do play a fearful tune, Alicia. However did you get to be shaped like a musical instrument?" Dormouse ran his tongue around the milk carton rim.

What big trouble! Having my name, photograph, email address, and hacker handle blasted across the Internet was as serious as having my identity stolen.

"You look scared, Alicia," Dormouse said and laughed.

7. The Dormouse Gets Me Lost

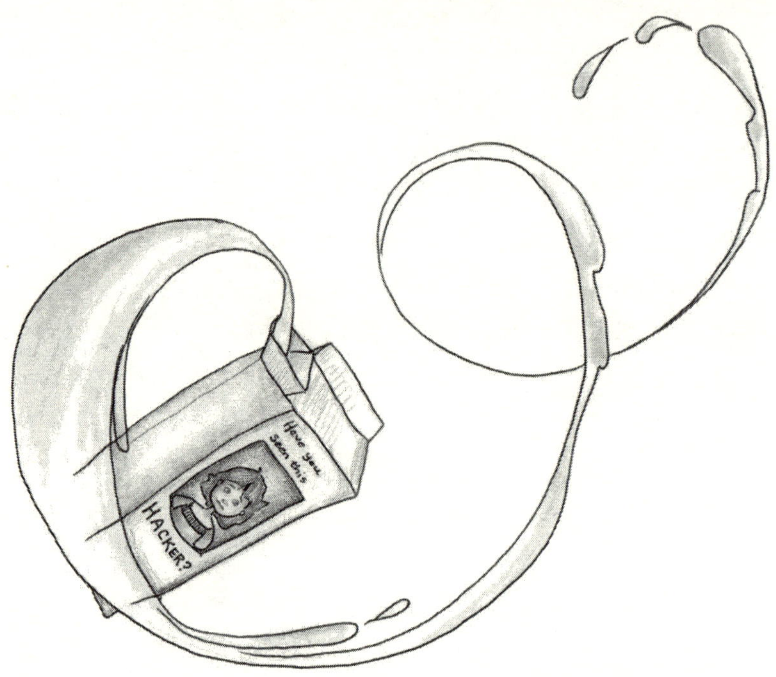

I flung my arm at the milk carton. The spout opened, pouring milk over my head. Like a wet paper doll, I folded to the floor, into a soaking pool of cream. My staircase folds straightened, proving Mom right—milk does build strong bones. Unfortunately, there was not enough milk left to beef up my muscles, so I was still flat, like a paper doll.

I shoved the milk carton, with my picture on it, under the table.

I picked at crumbs on the floor, stuffing them in my mouth and chewing silently. It took but a few crumbs to fill the stomach of a girl, tinier than a hummingbird.

My pocket was big enough to hold some crumbs of cheese for later.

Dormouse burped. He lifted his leg and farted, waving his hand around his rear end.

I held my nose.

"What? You think I stink?" he shouted. Dormouse threw his napkin on the floor and kicked the chair over.

He picked me up, sopping wet from milk.

Dormouse flung me from his pad.

I lay on the ground with my legs and arms twisted like pretzels, praying nothing tore.

"I kicked you out of my pad. Now you know what it feels like!" he screamed.

"You were voted out of the Chaos Computing Club, not kicked out. It was a Democratic process," I yelled.

"*It was Democracy*," he mimicked. "They don't teach social studies in third grade!"

Dormouse grabbed my wrists, dragging me across a yellow brick road.

I hollered, screamed, and kicked. My protest was useless because I was like a damp sheet of paper.

Do not cry in front of Dormouse, I thought. *Do not give the eight-year-old jerk the satisfaction! Chin up, Alicia. Just be careful not to rip your arm. Soon, you will dry.*

Dormouse stopped at a sign that read, *Cable Station*.

We zigzagged through a maze of rainbow-colored tracks. At the end were three cable cars, a white car, a grey car, and a black car.

He lugged me into the grey cable car, slamming the door and locking us both in.

My damp body slid from the bench to the floor.

Dormouse placed his shoe on my chest.

The car twirled around, hanging us upside down.

The car flipped back around and my stomach flopped.

"Where are we going?" I said, trying not to sound fearful.

"This car connects the monitor to the computer," he said.

I snapped my teeth, trying to bite his ankle.

He pinched my arm, causing a wrinkle on my soggy skin. Dormouse slumped against the seat but looked happy.

"I'm sorry my temper exploded. If this cable car takes us into the computer's guts, do you know your way back up to the monitor?"

"Why should I help you return when I can instead get you lost?" he said.

The cable car gave a jerk and we started moving.

Like a roller coaster, the cable car went down, around and up in circles through a long, twisted cable.

It seemed my stomach peeked from my ears before falling to my feet.

At last, the ride stopped and the doors opened.

I crawled from the cable car, moaning. My tummy felt like wires were sticking my intestines.

Dormouse spun dizzily on his tennis shoes. "We are inside the computer's guts. This is Cyber City where users in human forms are not welcome. There is a line, Alicia, and you crossed it. You broke the most major rule—respect the hardware," he said, gloating.

"Gnomes kidnapped me and now you force me to come here!" Yet, I was too awestruck for ill humor. History might record that I was the first human to be physically inside a computer. Cyber City was a stunning mecca of flashing neon lights. The buildings were shiny metal and glass, reflecting colored lights bouncing off each other like a laser show. Cobalt-blue lights pulsed above the city, passing for a sky. In between crackling noises, a pleasant sound hummed like a fan blowing a cool breeze.

Taking the wrong cable car had not been such a bad idea. Dad's file labeled, *Irresponsible Alicia,* was here, somewhere. An added benefit was that the wild ride in the twisted cable car acted like a spinning clothes dryer. I no longer walked like a wet dork but strutted with my chin held proudly.

Human-like creatures kept bumping into us without even a how-do-you-do or a pardon-me. They were shadowy avatars that moved quickly, except for the occasional avatar that stopped for a microsecond to examine me.

One avatar moved in a menacing way.

The avatar pounced, causing me to shriek.

Dormouse yanked us up a building.

I clung to his shoe and stuck out my tongue at the avatar below.

The walls were loose, and flapped as we climbed, causing the building to sway. What a relief to be away from those menacing shadows.

Dormouse climbed through a window of the 13th floor.

Dormouse knocked on a glass door with the name, *Computer File Room.* No one answered. He turned the handle, clicking his teeth nervously.

Trees sprouted in the room like a forest. Instead of leaves hanging from the branches, manila file folders dangled. Each file-tree had a nametag.

Books lined the walls, but the books were untouchable. Instead, my hand sunk into the wall. "These aren't real books, just pictures," I said, snorting. "Are there any hard walls in Cyber City?"

"Just wallpaper hangs between the rooms, for pretty," he said.

Files hung from the branches of a file-tree. I snapped off a folder with a label *Backup*. There were four envelopes in this heavy folder. Consequently, I emptied parts of the folder into the trash can before hanging the folder back on its file tree, since none of the files was of interest.

I kept picking off files, sorting through the contents and emptying some in the can. "I hope those weren't important," I mumbled. A file named *Recovery* lay atop the trash heap.

Bingo! *Irresponsible Alicia* was stamped on the label of a folder that drooped from a branch on the next tree.

I broke off the folder with care, and hugged it. "Mission accomplished. We can go now."

"Go where, flat head?" Dormouse said.

"Back up to the monitor, cheese brain."

He scratched his head. "Well if I'm a cheese brain, I have too many holes in my skull. Therefore, I can't remember the way back," he yelled.

"You are so not cool!" I hollered, boxing his nose.

Dormouse punched back with his bigger paws. He knocked me to the floor and stood over me, wiggling his whiskers.

"Getting us lost in the computer is flipping me out," I said.

"I am not lost, but you are a helpless fool without your avatar," Dormouse said.

He dug his claws into the wood of the desk and climbed with me dangling from one of his suspenders. With my other hand, I clung to the file.

Dormouse heaved us onto the desktop.

On the desktop was a winter wonderland. There was a dark-blue sky with white balls hanging above thick snow. A snow cone forest rose from the white ground.

Dormouse slid in the frozen snow. He tripped and knocked over an inkbottle. He hopped on one foot. "Gosh darn!" He plopped down, removed his tennis shoe, and striped sock. He clipped his toenail with his teeth, ripping away the jagged edges. He licked around his trimmed toenail to sand his nail smooth with his rough tongue.

Meanwhile, ink kept spilling from the bottle he had turned topsy-turvy. I tried to lift the bottle, but it was too heavy. I attempted to shove the cap on the bottle to stop the spill, but the bottle kept rolling. The dripping ink made the desktop resemble blue ice.

I wiped at the ink spot on the desktop with a tissue, but the spot got bigger. "Oh, well, an ink blot is like yesterday's newspaper," I said, tossing the tissue over my shoulder.

Bingo! The desktop is the *graphical user interface* or *GUI* for the computer. My way home is hidden in the link between my world and the cyber world, the desktop. *There must be a help menu*, I thought.

"You don't remember where you left things on the desktop!" I shouted.

"Yes, I do." Dormouse scurried to the other side of the desk and dived into a trash can. He dug in the trash, stuffing a half-eaten slice of spam in his mouth.

"Help me find the *help menu*, Dormouse," I yelled down at the trash can.

The little turd threw me a birdie.

How dare he throw a dirty finger, I thought. Huffing and puffing, I pushed a giant eraser across the desktop and over the side of the desk. The eraser landed dead center in the trash can.

Dormouse cursed until the last thing to be erased was his obnoxious mouth.

8. I Meet a Dictionary Named Merriam

There must be a *help menu* somewhere on the desktop. Under the snow was a basket marked, *Out Email.* I scribbled a letter on a scrap of paper. The letter read:

Dear Dad, please do not be angry. I am lost inside your computer and have become a virtual girl. It is not my fault that the beasties kidnapped me.

Love,

Your so responsible daughter, Alicia

I underlined the words, *so responsible,* with the color red and then dropped the letter in the *Out Email* basket.

Ping!

A yellow envelope addressed to *Alicia* popped into the *In Email* Basket. The sender cut each letter of my name from a magazine and glued the letters on crooked. My heart skipped at the thought that this must be a rescue email. Dormouse's toenail made a great letter opener. The email had two sentences: *We no who u r. We have been watching u.*

"Whoever you are, you need a spell checker," I bellowed. The email fit in my small pocket.

It was apparent Dad knew I was a spy because in the folder labeled, *Irresponsible Alicia,* he used big words. Did I tell you that computer hackers are lousy spellers with small vocabularies because we write in scripting languages to break into computers? The Internet is a secret tunnel to dig our way through, one keyboard stroke at a time. We write script programs to run as fast as lightning, guessing at passwords. We steal login names or deduce a login from stolen files. Oops, I mean borrowed files.

"I would give *anything* for a dictionary," I hollered.

Presto, a dictionary emerged in the file room. "Maid Merriam here, unabridged dictionary." Maid Merriam was dressed rather smartly in white shoes, white gloves, and a top hat. Imagine my surprise to find out that the dictionary was a she.

"What is the formal meaning of ir-res-pon-si-ble?" I said, pronouncing each syllable.

Her gold-leaf pages flapped as the dictionary spoke in a fluttery voice. "First, hand over your ballet shoes."

"These are dancing shoes, you silly book."

"I am merely a collector. I shall not dance with your shoes. Exercise bends the spine, though Yoga helps loosen my pages." The dictionary posed in a pretzel-like yoga pose.

"Wow! You can do yoga because you are a digital book and not made of paper."

"We shall play Scrabble for your shoes," Merriam said.

"I am not stupid enough to play Scrabble with a dictionary."

"Perhaps you are mad enough then. My top hat, I won it playing Scrabble with a mad hatter."

"I would be nuts to play Scrabble with a dictionary. Just do your job and define the word *irresponsible*."

"You said, you would give *anything* for my help," Merriam said.

I grabbed the dictionary around her middle, trying to turn her pages.

Merriam kicked and slapped.

I forced her pages open to the letter *i*.

Merriam snapped her book cover closed.

"Ouch! You nearly bit off my fingers!" I said.

Merriam stood in a fighting pose with her pages open to the word, *karate*.

"Humph! Rather than surrender my ballet shoes, I shall make my best educated guess."

Merriam's pages flew to the letter *G*, for glasses. She removed a pair of reading glasses from the page, placing them on the tip of her nose. She scanned me from head to toe. Her pages bolted to the letter *C,* and her book cover slammed with a bang. "I knew it! You are a *cheater*," she said.

"And you are a dumb dictionary. My ballet shoes are not *anything*. The shoes are not a thing because the shoes are a pair and so plural. What is the use of a dictionary, if it has no grammar?"

"You think you have troubles? Within my pulp, every English word squabbles. The *adverbs* wish to spend qualify time with the *verbs*, but the *verbs* are looking for more action. The *synonyms* oppose the *antonyms* and declared war. The *nouns* are jealous of the *pronouns* and just this morning, armed themselves with spoons and soup. The *nouns* now threaten to drown the *pronouns* in chicken noodle. The *indefinite* articles have become more particular than the *definite* articles. Meanwhile, the *negative* articles depressed the *zero* articles. The zeros jumped off my pages, taking the holes in *mathematics* with them. The *adjectives* are so powerful that they threaten revolt to form a *thesaurus*. And you, mad user, grow curiouser and curiouser," Merriam said.

"Give the meaning of *irresponsible*, or I'll find matches for a book burning party!"

"Tut, tut, child! Every word has a definition, if only you can find it."

I grabbed her back and front covers, trying to pry her open.

Merriam kept her spine clamped shut.

"First, your shoes," she said, snapping her fingers.

I removed the ballet shoes from around my neck and handed the pair to Merriam.

The dictionary's feet were too small for my shoes. She pulled tissues for shoe stuffing from her *Ti* page.

Merriam twirled on my ballet shoes. "How do I look?"

"Like a silly romance novel."

"I am not a silly romance, although an encyclopedia did break my heart last year."

"If you wanted a pair of ballet shoes, why not just remove a pair from your pages?" I said.

"Because I wanted your shoes to see if you could dance, but you are a silly dancer," she said.

"I fulfilled my part of our bargain," I said.

"I refuse to help a silly dancer. Silly! Silly!" she screamed.

I shoved Merriam.

The dictionary fell sideways on the snowy desktop. She kicked her legs like a bug turned upside down. The dictionary was open to the letter *R*. "Quick! Help me to right myself, before *rhyme* and *reason* escape," she shrieked.

"Yes, I'm sure *rhyme* and *reason* want to be freed from your mad pages," I said.

Merriam was heavy from the weight of every English word. Nevertheless, I pushed the dictionary back on its legs. "Is *thank you* defined in your pages?" I said, glaring.

"Phrases are not," Merriam said. She fluttered to the letter *i*. "*Irresponsible* means, not being responsible," she said, spitting ink from her pages.

"What is the use defining all that stuff, if you don't explain it as you go on? *Irresponsible* is by far the most confusing word ever defined," I said.

"Well then, we must dig for the word's *root* and find a better definition," she said. Merriam flapped her pages to the letter *R*. "*Responsible* means, being to blame for something as in, who is *responsible* for deleting Louse-the-Mouse and the hacker known as Dormouse?"

"You're making that example up about the mouses! According to your definition of *responsible*, I can't be *irresponsible*, because I am *responsible* for erasing Dormouse, who erased Louse-the-Mouse," I said, sniffling.

She flipped her pages to the letter *K*. "Well in that case, *karma* is responsible for erasing Dormouse, who erased Louse-the-Mouse. This all means that you are *irresponsible Alicia*."

"What are you writing on the *i* page?" I shrieked.

"I am recording a glowing example of *irresponsible*. I have made you famous. All the online dictionaries will now use you as an example of *irresponsible*."

"No," I screamed. "I must prove that I'm responsible!"

"Ta-ta then, and break a leg!" Merriam waved her pinky.

"Wait! Do not leave me stranded here. There must be some word in your dictionary that can help."

"I am late for a beauty pageant which is why I needed to learn ballet." Merriam twirled clumsily on my slippers. "Goodbye human, virtual girl, stupid user, bad dancer, avatar, gnome hunter, cheater, whatever you are. My *synonyms* are going nuts, loony, crazy, and insane trying to describe you. One mob swears you are a *mop head*, while another insists you are a *Christmas tree,* layered on top with dull tinsel. The *adjectives* argue that you are a *baking pan,* because two biscuits connect your calves to your thighs."

"Those biscuits are knees," I said.

"The *nouns* bicker that you are a *vegetable*, since your bottom limbs are carrots. An opposing group protests that you must be a *flower*, because petals fan from your four stems."

"My petals are fingers and toes," I said, wiggling my digits.

"But your bottom petals move like *pedals* so I disagree with all camps. I am the queen of words," Merriam said, haughtily. She placed a hand on my head, bestowing a title. "I declare you a *bicycle* due to that tire around your middle."

Another tip regarding computers: if you have to use a dictionary, never argue with the book—she will always have the last word, unless you push her.

Merriam lost her balance. She toppled into the file trees. "You should throw your words gently, dear," the dictionary said.

There was a noise from the desktop. The snow cones moved.

"Eek! Gnomes," Merriam screamed.

The snow cones stood, revealing legs. Hiding beneath them were gnomes.

The dictionary fluttered its pages, throwing nouns, mainly pots, pans, plates, saucers, and a Scrabble game.

Pouf! The dictionary vanished.

The gnomes ran on their pointy shoes, slipping and sliding. The beasties resembled Santa's elves dressed in red and green sticky-note snowsuits held together with paper clips. The gnomes doubled up the sticky-notes for warmth. Still their shiny lips froze to their snowy moustaches. They grinned with vampire-like teeth.

Snow flew everywhere, unburying a map. The map had a *C Drive, D Drive, E Drive* and other letters. Even better, a square on the map read, *HOME*.

Flying gnomes sang repeatedly, "March on the right path and by March, you will have marched so far, you will be marching back the way you came."

It was April, and March was eleven months away! There must be a shortcut. "Which road is the right path to *HOME*?" I said, biting my nails. "Oh, the gnomes are getting closer!"

The map resembled a flat Monopoly game token. I jumped on a square that read *STARTUP*, and then screamed when the square moved towards a square named *SHUTDOWN*. I backed away from *SHUTDOWN,* but *STARTUP* changed directions, hovering in the air next to a brick labeled *RESTART*.

Eek! Gnomes chopped off five bricks on one of the paths towards *HOME*.

Each time I ran down a path, gnomes hacked the squares in half with teensy-weensy snow shovels, while singing. Gnomes chopped off every path until *HOME* floated on an iceberg, out of my reach. Surrounding the iceberg were snow cones, as if the gnomes never revealed themselves.

9. I Ride a Trojan Horse

The sound of heavy boots clobbered towards the room. Someone yelled out in a German accent, "We are coming for you, White-Rabbit! I mean, Alicia!"

I tripped on the *Help* key of a calculator, slid on its *Backspace* key, and tumbled off the desktop. I bounced on a leaf pile in the trash can, flew up, and landed on the floor.

The door handle slowly turned.

I pushed the swinging door on a file-tree with a name tag, *Garden,* and walked into a cool, spring scene. This room was made of wallpaper with sunflowers, daisies, and multi-colored roses growing on the walls.

I climbed to the bluest daisy and plopped down in the middle of the flower. Mom smelled a lot like a daisy. She must be getting home from her nursing job about now. Mom had such soothing hands. One time, a boy at school broke my heart. Mom hugged me and said, "The world isn't ending, Sweetheart."

It seemed my world had ended. "The difference between me and these flowers is that they will bloom next spring, whereas I..."

A Cuckoo Bumblebee hovered in front of my nose. Some Cuckoos live in New Mexico and California, but this Cuckoo had not heard the war was over. The bee wore red flying goggles and a brown, World-War-I-leather flying cap. The bee rakishly flung an orange scarf around his neck. His antennas were wires. His wings were a rainbow's colors, with sparks of light when he fluttered about. He had two fangs, from which yellow goo dripped. He buzzed with a thick lisp against my ear.

The Cuckoo twirled through the air, spelling words like an airplane. *Your pollen tastes yucky*, the bee spelled.

"That's not pollen in my ear; it's wax."

He sucked on my cheek and then spelled, *U r an odd flour. Your pollen tastes salty.*

"Those are my tears you've tasted, you Cuckoo Bumblebee. Go away, and leave me alone!"

Bye jovey! U r a daisy, the bee spelled. He slapped his forehead with his metal arm. A dent caved in his head between his hundreds of eyes.

"I'm not a daisy. I'm an Alicia."

Alicia, the sour-tasting flour, he spelled.

"And you are Cuckoo, the bumbler bee who cannot spell."

Know. U r wrong. Eye am a spelling bee, he said, drawing flashy words in the air. *Eye nose how too spell reel good. Eye bee a spill chequer, 2 catch a user miss steaks. Weather Eye am write oar wrong, rarely dew eye maid mist aches.*

"Well, I have often seen a spelling bee; but a bee spelling? You have spelled wordless sentences. Are you a hacker?" I said suspiciously because Bumbler could not spell.

I help u, Cuckoo spelled, spinning somersaults in the air.

"Show-off," I said and smiled.

The bee hung upside down, flapping his wings. He pointed at the window with one antenna.

"Oh, alright." I jumped off the daisy and followed Cuckoo to the window.

The bee banged his nose against the glass. "Bzz. Bz. Z." He crashed to the floor appearing unconscious.

The Cuckoo was a spell checker for the computer and therefore, a program. "Program crash. Restart," I yelled, counting, "One. Two. Three."

"Z. Bz. Bzz." Cuckoo flew around the room and then once more, banged his nose on the glass.

"Get out, pest," I said, opening the window.

Cuckoo flew out the window, landing on the ear of a wooden horse, whose head reached the 13th floor window.

In Greek Mythology, the Trojans used a similar, giant wooden horse to rescue a beautiful girl. I spit on my fingers and pulled at my hair to try to comb it.

I grabbed onto the horse's ears and slid down its neck, bouncing on the saddle. I was a pocket-sized girl on a massive horse, hoping to look more lovely than nerdy.

The wooden horse turned its head and winked.

"Are you a Trojan horse?" I said.

"I'm a sick Trojan," he said through stiff lips, sounding like a cowboy.

"I'm homesick myself," I said.

"I'm not sick of home. I just carry a virus," the Trojan said.

"I'm homesick for the real world. You're so pretty," I said, patting his mane. "We must find you a virtual veterinarian to cure your virus."

The Trojan whinnied, rolling down the street on wooden, squealing wheels.

Cuckoo flew out the horse's ear landing, stinger down, on its rump.

The Trojan screamed, spinning its wheels down the street at high speed.

"Yi," I yelled, slipping and grabbing onto a rope hanging from the saddle.

The rope gave way and the wooden horse's hollow belly snapped open. A pack of chariots zoomed out its stomach. On each chariot rode a gnome, buggy-red-eyed, with sharp teeth and runny noses. The gnomes were dressed like Trojan warriors with feathered helmets, red skirts, and capes. Sandals crisscrossed their short legs. They held their shields in front of them, waving their swords and screaming, "Bloody war!"

The Trojan-gnomes paid no attention to me. They all stared intently ahead, like gnomes on a mission.

A pack of fleas flew behind the gnomes. Their wings were long. The fleas let off a powerful stink as they flew in formation, like bomber planes, in the direction of *Cyber City*.

The Trojan-gnomes snapped their whips at the chariots to fly faster.

The gnomes and fleas became mere specks in the sky.

The Trojan belched, feeling better now that its nasty stomachache had flown from its belly.

The horse wheeled away with me still swinging from the rope.

My arms were weakening. There was about a thirteen-story distance to the ground.

Cuckoo lifted his stinger from the rump of the Trojan horse.

The horse swished its tail at a gang of fleas on its back.

A flea fell on Cuckoo. "Bzzzzz," the bee hissed.

The flea flew away with a bit of Cuckoo hanging from its mouth.

Cuckoo brushed his wings against my leg.

"Stop or you'll make me let go of this rope. I shall break my virtual head then. Spell, *escape this mess*," I said, kicking at the bee.

The stubborn Cuckoo hovered beneath, until I wrapped my legs around his back. The bee's body felt furry soft. His wire antennas vibrated in my hands.

We flew through the Trojan's legs whose wheels were screeching downhill.

10. I Crash a Mad, Mad Java Party

Cuckoo flew into a cloud, shaped like a coffee pot. We poured from the cloud's spout, through a flowered archway, into a garden surrounded by a white picket fence. Singing birds perched on statues. Rainbows shot from fountains. Except for holes littering the garden, this place looked like paradise.

Incoming, Cuckoo spelled with wiggly lines, before skidding to a stop on a table. He banged his antennas against a coffee pot labeled, *Java Virtual Machine*. The machine churned away, Java spitting from the spigot. Java is the most powerful programming language. Java trickled across the table, staining the tablecloth black.

Identical twins, with square heads, hunkered at the head of the table. They dressed alike, with high starched collars and choking, bow ties. Their beady eyes hid behind wire-rimmed glasses. Their names were sewn proudly on tweed jackets. The twins had enormous ears and were identical, except for two differences. One twin had his head screwed on backward. His name was *Illogic*. His brother's name was *Logic*. Logic smoked a pipe, but Illogic had a pipe sticking out of his left ear, dripping with earwax.

"Well, Cuckoo, we see you have arrived with your usual, clumsy flair," Logic said.

"Exception," Illogic screamed. "You have arrived with your usual fare, Cuckoo!" Illogic slapped himself. "There is no fare; the Java party is free. Not free! Flee," he shrieked in a panicked voice. Illogic whipped his head back, flinging his chair over. He wrestled with his legs to keep them from running away.

"My brother tried to divide by zero too many times," Logic said. He switched his brother's full cup of Java, with his own empty cup. Logic sipped the Java, rattling his cup against the plate. His head twitched. Like his brother, his face was long and thin. His crew-cut hairstyle shaped his head like a block.

"I knew it! Blockheads," I said.

"We are heads of the block, and we did not invite you to our block party, daisy," Logic said.

"Like I told Cuckoo, I am not a daisy," I said.

"*Like I told Cuckoo, I am not a daisy,*" Logic mimicked. "Then go, daisy. We allow only artificial intelligence at our party."

"Then why is a block of wood here?" I said.

"Because this is a block party," Illogic screeched.

The block of wood wore a baseball cap. It was a lump of bocote wood with streaks, creating a lizard-like face. It had swirls of eyes at each top corner and a bump centered at the top. The block of wood resembled an earless Yoda with wrinkles of woody lines. Like all exotic woods, the block glowed with the loneliness of an alien.

"The block of wood is a block of programming code. Blocky is a great thinker." Logic whispered as if he reported a golf shot. "We wait as Blocky tees wisdom off his brain."

Blocky spoke with an Australian accent. "How ya goin', Mates? No smokin' allowed or matches. We want no fires. G'day, Mates," it said. Glue dribbled from cracks in its wood.

Logic puffed on his pipe, swirling smoke around Blocky.

The block of wood coughed.

"If Blocky's words are so wise, why don't you follow the wood's advice and not smoke?" I said.

"I don't smoke. My pipe smokes." Logic set his pipe to rest on Blocky. The pipe glowed red.

Illogic smacked my hand away from the cookie jar. "Exception! As you can see, there is not enough food. Yuck. Yuck," he said.

"Why, there's enough food to feed an army," I said.

"There is enough food to feed an army," Illogic said. He snapped his fingers, and ants parachuted from the sky, hundreds landing on the table. The ants wore army helmets and four pairs of combat boots. One ant played the trumpet, and another the drums. The ants resembled plain red ants, except with a pig's snout.

The ants marched in tune, toward the food.

"The picnic is for the army ants," Illogic said.

"Why, that's harebrained, giving a picnic for ants," I said.

Logic wagged his finger. "Tut-tut. This ant army is the anti-virus, programmed to fight the computer virus that has infected the world. The army will march off in a WAR file. Combat is their program."

"This may be their last meal," Illogic said.

An ant, with four plastic stars glued to his helmet, clicked his combat boots together. "We are ready to attack, and await your orders," the ant said, saluting Logic.

"Go ahead, General Ant, the feast is all yours," Logic said, saluting him back.

The ants sounded like pigs as their snout noses moved through the food like vacuum cleaners.

Cuckoo buzzed around the table, dipping into Java cups. The black stuff dripped from his fangs, staining his scarf.

Logic poked my back with a fork, scooting me to the end of the table where a big-bellied beetle, dressed in a fancy pinstriped suit, sat. "If you must stay, then be seated. We sit from the head to the foot of the table, according to class. You may be seated at the lowest end, daisy," Logic said. He spoke with his thin nose in the air with a snotty, British accent.

"Quit stabbing me with your fork! Stop calling me lower class, you freaky avatar! I'm not a daisy," I said, kicking the table.

The beetle winked. "And none of us is avatars, including you. Trust me to keep my mouth shut, User." The bug spoke through the side of his mouth, like a gangster. A cigar hung from his lip. Like Cuckoo, his antennas were wires, but bent. His legs were created from hairy wires. The hair on his legs gave off flashes of colored light.

"Do I look so much like a user?" I said in a small voice.

"You've got that lost face about you, like you're overwhelmed by technology," the bug said.

"Oh, but I'm a..."

"Hacker? I know," the bug said and farted. "Being a hacker ain't the same thing as virtual."

"I appear lost because this is my first time as a virtual girl, inside the computer. None of you like users?" I whispered.

The bug leaned back in his chair and smiled lazily, puffing on a cigar. "Envy often leads to dislike, don't it? You and I have more in common than you think."

"I have nothing in common with a computer bug," I said.

"A single program does not limit us, as it does them." The bug pointed his antennae to the others at the Java party. A figure appearing like the Grim Reaper reclined on the right side of the table. She wore a raggedy-hooded, black robe, and black mask. A teensy man sat opposite Grim Reaper. The tiny man had a huge balloon-head attached to his long spaghetti-neck.

"Hopefully she won't lose her temper," I said, eyeing the blood-specked scythe. Grim Reaper's face was just a shadow with eyes. She cursed when she tried to eat a cookie.

"Ignore Grim Reaper and her bad temper. The Reaper is berserk because she will never drink a cup of Java because she has no mouth. Her job is executions in the *City of Memory Chips*."

I raised an eyebrow at the tiny man with the heart-shaped balloon-head, waving about his threadlike neck. The balloon head was transparent pink, displaying a pea-sized brain.

"That is Oxy-Moron, a thesaurus. The virus killed off all his synonyms and left the antonyms."

Oxy-Moron tried to drink warm water, but a breeze blew his head about the glass. He raised his glass. "Let us toast to our affluent poverty!" His balloon head jiggled like a car dashboard figure with a springy neck. "Thank you for calling, and have a nice day," he said in an East Indian customer-service voice.

"Can you help me?" I whispered to Stinky.

"Bugs only help themselves," he said.

"They're crazy," I said, pointing my chin to the twins.

"We're all mad here. This place has become an insane asylum since the virus," the bug said.

"Everyone's fighting over cups of Java, yet there's plenty to go around."

"Human beings are made up of 70% water. The smartest cyber beings are programmed with 100% Java," he said.

"I've never seen Java that color," I said, wrinkling my nose at the purple, red and blue striped coffee, spitting from the machine.

"Red in the Java programming language is pesticide, which makes it hard for computer bugs like me, who break programs. I'm the best though," he said.

The bug jumped on the table, balancing on the longest of his six spaghetti legs. He rubbed his antennas together. His pinstriped suit transformed to a formal tuxedo. Even with silk, top hat, and tails, the beetle was gross. Bags puffed beneath his eyes. His face was flushed grey, with blisters and boils covering his skin. A jagged knife scar cut his face in half. He did have a wonderful voice though. The beetle tap-danced across the table, carrying a golden cane beneath his arm, and singing.

"I want a lazy programmer,
No error checking so the program I can freeze.
Give me a hazy programmer,
One who cannot see the forest for the trees.
Oh, where is the crazy programmer?
One with no logic, please.
Oh, where? Oh where? Have the buffalo..."

He leaned on his cane, tipped his hat, and bowed.

Did he actually expect me to clap? "You haven't finished your song."

"I stole just a snippet of *Dancing with the Stars At Home* program," he said. The bug shrugged his hunched back. "Somewhere, out there, is a dance program which starts at the end and has no beginning. The song is fragmented because of my talents. I also put a toad in the program, so the singing sounds like Koimit, the froggy."

"Oh, that is funny," I said, clapping.

The bug farted and laughed at me burying my nose in a napkin. "My breakfast smells good, don't it? I ate part of a program that spits out a recipe for boiled eggs," he said.

"Stinky," I said, pinching my nose.

The bug shook his fist and snarled, "How do you know my name? Did Moles snitch?"

"Moles do not confide in me. I never use a Mole for hacking. I am not a friend of Moles. I'm your friend, Stinky," I said, smiling and lying. A computer bug might be useful.

"Good cause I wanna be your friend. A user with hacking skills could come in handy. You and I could be soul mates." Stinky rubbed my leg with his creepy antennae. The bug's eyes turned all soft and mushy.

I never had a boyfriend but confess to a crush on the hacker Zebra. I admire big horsey teeth. Now, a bug is attracted to me. Antennas in a boyfriend are a big turnoff though. I mean, what would Justin Bieber think if my ex-boyfriend was a beetle? It was in the best interest of my future to cool Stinky's ardor. Therefore, I changed the subject.

"Speaking of Moles, what is he doing here," I whispered. Moles usually attack the Internet, yet a Mole ran past us in a hurry.

Stinky said, "I ain't afraid of moles. I covered my tracks with so much spaghetti code, no hacker will ever exploit me with a Mole or Worm or anything else."

The avatar of a hacker who goes by the handle Hedgehog joined the Mole. Hedgehog used to be a member of Chaos Computing Club but believed we were not creating enough chaos.

Stinky burped, rubbing his big belly. "It's that heartburn program I took a byte out of yesterday, White-Rabbit."

The bug said my hacker handle while Hedgehog spoke into a cell phone! Hedgehog was only eleven but left Chaos Computing and went over to the dark side of the web. He hung out in bad areas of the Internet at trashy online clubs. Ghost hackers recruited the kid. The specialty of a Ghost hacker is to utilize Moles to burrow through a user's web browser while the user surfs the Internet. Have you ever gotten a computer virus after surfing to a web page? It was probably a Ghost hacker.

A RAT sat on a rock with the Mole and Hedgehog! A RAT is a Remote Administration Tool used by some hackers. For example, the GhostNet hackers use a RAT to steal emails in order to access email addresses. A GhostNet hacker can then gain real-time control of an addressee's computer, using the RAT.

The RAT lifted its nose, sniffing.

I rubbed cookie crumbs on the email stuffed in my pocket to disguise its scent. Hedgehog was still on the phone. The Mole began running around in circles as if agitated. RAT must be going on a long, remote trip. It carried a traveling bag.

What exactly were these three up to?

11. I Dance for my Supper

Illogic dug a hole in the garden, muttering something about, "gnome treasure." He threw dirt on the table across the food. His pants had quite a few byte marks on the cloth. A piece of cloth, the same color, hung from the bug's mouth. The beetle chewed, swallowed, and burped. "I promise not to tell your secret about being a human. Honor among crooks," Stinky said.

"I'm not a crook," I hissed.

"Ain't you? Breaking and entering? Rubbing out Louse?"

"Dormouse rubbed out Louse."

"And what happened to Dormouse?" The bug posed one antennae in a question mark.

"Sh! I didn't know the eraser would, well, you know."

"Oh, cripes, you rubbed out your navigator," the bug said, laughing so hard tears ran down his cheeks.

Illogic plopped down between us. Illogic and Stinky put their heads together and spoke softly.

"The daisy looks too familiar," Illogic said.

"Her face is on a milk carton," Stinky said.

"She is a saltine," Illogic said, slapping his head.

"I am not a cracker," I yelled.

"Shut up, saltine!" Illogic said in a shrill voice. "You crackered your way in here. You cracker your way into soup. Bring a straw to drink this soda cracker!" Illogic jumped behind me, poking my head with a straw. He slurped some strands of my hair.

"That hurts! I hope you choke."

Illogic pinched me. "You aren't a very nice daisy."

"What's the reward for a cracker these days?" Stinky said.

"Becoming an icon on the desktop," Illogic said.

Stinky pounded his fist on the table. "I need to be an icon on the computer screen, so users can click my pretty face, and break their programs. I gotta win that reward, before the Gnome King gets her."

"What Gnome King?" I said and gulped.

Illogic said, "I'll split the reward with you, Stinky. We will get a scam going. No! A spam! We will use email to spam that Computer Land has been crackered! I have crackered up! They're coming to take me away to the crazy house!" Illogic hugged his legs that were furiously kicking the air, trying to escape.

A pounding noise came from carpenter ants, who were building a stage.

Logic snapped his fingers, and a microphone rose in his hand. His clothes changed to a white tuxedo. "Before we entertain the troops, who are to battle the virus, I'll loosen up the crowd with a joke. What is the last line written in the User Manual?

"Customer support's phone number and a credit card number request," I yelled.

"What is the last lifeline written in the User Manual, bro?" Logic repeated and pointed to his brother.

"In case of an emergency landing, your laptop can be used as a flotation device!" Illogic said.

They all found the joke funny. I slumped in my chair, not even laughing when the block of wood changed into a pig.

Logic rocked the pig like a baby, and then threw the pig at his brother.

Illogic caught the snorting pig. He dumped a gallon of pepper on the pig. "Pepper for the pig! More pepper!" he shouted. "We must season the main course!"

"Should we season the pig with summer, winter, spring, or fall?" Stinky yelled.

"Beat the pig, if it sneezes," Grim Reaper snarled, pounding her scythe on the ground.

The shaking earth woke some caterpillars, who slinked from their garden beds. One caterpillar sat on the pig with a straw hat shading it from the sun.

Suddenly, a message appeared written in smoke:

I spun around but could see no friendly face.

A caterpillar crawled up my arm. This caterpillar wore computer glasses and smoked a hookah pipe. His big nose kept his owl-like glasses from falling off his face.

"Oh, it's you," I whispered back with huge relief.

Caterpillar sat on my shoulder and took a puff of his pipe. "I was waiting for an opportunity to hack in. Hello, White-Rabbit," he whispered in a voice sounding wise like Yoda from *Star Wars*. Indeed, Caterpillar hummed the theme song from the movie.

"Hello," I said. Here was rescue, at last. It took all my control not to kiss Caterpillar, but that would be weird.

"I have something important to say," he said. Caterpillar cleared his throat of a few clods of dirt. "Keep your temper else you might lose your head," he said, very businesslike.

"Is that all you have to say?" I squeaked.

"No. You received an email earlier," Caterpillar said, puffing on his pipe.

"That was you?"

"No," Caterpillar said, blowing smoke in my face.

"Then what?" I said, coughing.

Thinking always caused wrinkles on Caterpillar's face to deepen. "There was something important. Ah, yes. What could you do with an email and RAT?"

"I could gain control of a computer and all its peripherals, such as the camera and speakers," I said.

"What computer could you gain control of?"

"With the email in my pocket addressed to me, and a Remote Administration Tool, I could gain control of my computer. Did you send the RAT to help me?"

"No, but what is the probability of a RAT, Mole and Hedgehog being together at a Java party?"

"The RAT must be up to no good. The hard part will be enticing the RAT to abandon his friends, the Mole and Hedgehog," I said.

Caterpillar's voice suddenly changed from wise, ancient Yoda to a boy. "Oops! Sorry, but I have no more time to solve your problems. My mom is calling me for breakfast. We are going out of town to visit an aunt who lives in the mountains with no Internet access. I got a dirt bike yesterday for my 13th birthday. If you ever get out of this mess, maybe we can take another online vacation. We should race cars over the Swiss Alps."

"Neat!"

"Bye, Alicia. Nice knowing who you really are."

"Wait! You know my real name. What is *your* real name?"

"Ah, now that is a riddle," Caterpillar said, leaving behind some smoke.

There were two caterpillars staring at the stage, and then four, and then eight caterpillars, etc. The caterpillars were duplicating themselves. They were really worms created by a hacker.

The worms crawled away, no doubt headed for a network of computers, so each could infect one.

Caterpillar reappeared sitting on my shoulder. "I forgot to remove the worm I used to hack in."

Ping! Caterpillar and the worms vanished before I could even wish Caterpillar a nice vacation biking down the mountains.

"And now, for what you've all been waiting for, the entertainment!" Logic yanked open purple, velvet curtains hanging from the stage.

How odd, the stage is a jewelry box. There is even a mirror, I thought.

The spotlight moved from the empty stage, to me. "You must entertain us, daisy." The twins pushed me up the steps to the jewelry box.

"But the dictionary has my ballet slippers!" I objected.

"Break a leg!" they all yelled.

"Break your right leg," Logic added.

"Break you left leg," Illogic said.

Everyone sat stiffly eying the stage through binoculars, even Grim Reaper.

"Play the music to *Swan Lake*," I said in a voice filled with stage fright.

"You may not use helper programs, cheater," the twins hollered.

With one foot wobbling against my leg, I balanced on the toe of my tennis shoe. I lifted my hands above my head, posing like the ballerina doll in my jewelry box. However, my flattened body resembled a ballet paper doll—the amazing Alicia, dancer extraordinaire.

I twisted my hands above my head and spun in a circle. At first, it felt odd standing on the toe of my sneaker, twirling around to no music. Soon my troubles were forgotten with the excitement of performing. I imagined dancing on a grand stage, with Mom and Dad sitting in the audience.

Poof! I toppled and landed on my butt.

Ouch! The audience threw flowerless, thorny stems. There were murmurs about "program crashes," "bugs," and "drink more Java."

"It's not my fault! I have never practiced on a spinning stage. I am a trooper though, and the show must go on." I lifted my trembling chin, and stood like a statue. A haunting tune played, and the disk turned.

The song suddenly changed to an old Sinatra tune. The crooner's voice blared from speakers hidden in the trees: "Call me irresponsible. Call me unreliable. Throw in undependable, too..."

The disk quit turning, and hurled me from the stage. I landed next to the *Java Virtual Machine*, banging my head.

"That performance doesn't deserve any supper," Logic added.

"Her legs are weak since she hasn't eaten," Stinky yelled from the audience.

"Let her eat cake then," Illogic ordered.

Grim Reaper and Stinky each grabbed me by an arm. They dragged me to the table, plopping me down on a chair.

Logic banged a cake plate on the table. A note leaned against a slice of carrot cake. The note read, *laced with irresponsibility. Eat me.*

"Never!" I cried.

Grim Reaper and Stinky both held me down, while the twins force-fed me every letter of the word *irresponsibility*.

I vomited the letters *i* and *r,* which left just *responsibility* in my intestines. My stomach rumbled and an enormous burp erupted from my mouth. "Excuse me, but *responsibility* disagrees with me."

They all threw their cups and saucers, shouting, "You are very funny, Alicia, though you have no humor."

Oxy-Moron shouted, "Friendly-fire approaches."

It was the nasty fleas and Trojan-gnomes flying over the Java party, in bomber formation.

The Trojan-gnomes leaned over their chariots, throwing green-slime bombs. They struck Logic and he collapsed, next to a pile of party favors.

The army ants fired their weapons, but were no match for the fleas and Trojan-gnomes.

Grim Reaper, Illogic and Stinky, were the only ones left dancing on the table. Illogic danced a do-si-do with Stinky. Grim Reaper jumped with the Java Beans and army ants.

Trojan-gnomes parachuted from their chariots, the beasties joining the party. They performed a dance, kicking their sandals and twirling their shields.

The RAT? Where is the RAT? Ah, there he is, making his escape with the Mole.

The virus struck Hedgehog. He lay face down on the grass, slowly vanishing. I could just imagine the hacker, whose avatar Hedgehog represented, rebooting his computer, and hoping to be in time to rejoin the Mole and RAT who were making their escape in a rowboat.

A hand reached out and yanked a carrot from the cake, including the roots and dirt.

"Hello, Alicia, Caterpillar sent me to help," a voice said, followed by the sound of a crunching carrot.

I turned and looked into the face of my avatar, White-Rabbit.

12. An Avatar Helps Me

“Do you like my outfit?” White-Rabbit said. “My purse matches my hair bow.”

Never dress you avatar in a different outfit each hacking session. White-Rabbit had become vain and cunning. The look in her eyes said I had better compliment her or else. "You look lovely," I hastily said, smiling brightly. The RAT was going to get away, but White-Rabbit insisted on showing off her clothes and listing all the designers. It was my fault for always choosing different outfits for White-Rabbit and turning her into a fashion bunny monster.

"The RAT and Mole are leaving," I mumbled.

"Yes," White-Rabbit said, rotating her eyes while keeping her face foreword. Like a real rabbit, she could see in a near-complete circle, except for one blind spot in front of her nose. Therefore, White-Rabbit could see behind her. White-Rabbit had a very good security system and was very useful for hacking.

She wiggled her nose disapprovingly. "The RAT's pants are torn and stained. He's dressed like a beggar!"

"Well, he is a rat, after all."

"No fashion sense. See if you can keep up!" White-Rabbit hopped across the fields chasing the RAT and Mole.

My human speed was clearly a disadvantage. It was an odd relationship, me not being in control of White-Rabbit with a mouse or joystick. My avatar was telling me what to do.

Here is a tip involving avatars: Never let your avatar choose its own outfit else, the avatar will feel empowered to do what it wishes.

White-Rabbit's trail consisted of shells of sunflower seeds.

Suddenly, the ground shook with a powerful thumping.

Bingo! White-Rabbit found her prey. White-Rabbit hid behind a bend of electrical wires. The avatar stood frozen, watching the Mole digging a hole. The freezing was bunny behavior at the sight of danger.

"The mole is letting another RAT into the computer," White-Rabbit whispered.

A smaller RAT climbed out of the hole the Mole was digging.

"Perhaps the Mole and RAT will vanish in the hole the Mole is tunneling underground," I said.

"If that happens, we'll never find them," White-Rabbit said.

"The Mole has itty-bitty eyes hidden by its fur. It's a European Mole," I noted, "so the Mole has photopic vision. It's so bright in here from all the neon lights that the Mole might see us."

White-Rabbit snapped open a parasol matching her purse. "Here. I'll distract the Mole and then you shade the light to blind him with this parasol."

"Moles hear at low frequencies," I said.

Luckily, the Mole's digging was making a lot of noise so the Mole did not hear us sneak up on him. We stretched our necks to make sure we were not low to the ground where Moles hear well.

White-Rabbit tapped the Mole on its back. "You have decent shoes, but you should at least wear pants," she said.

I lifted the parasol, shading the Mole from the light.

"Who's there?" The Mole held out his hands as if he could not see.

At the speed of a blink, White-Rabbit kicked the Mole in the hole.

I quickly threw dirt in the hole, burying the Mole.

While I chased the smaller RAT, White-Rabbit surprised the large RAT who was sleeping.

The big RAT growled and gnashed its teeth while White-Rabbit placed it in shackles.

I was gentler with the smaller RAT.

White-Rabbit was ruthless with the big RAT. She considered the RATs predators since the rodents are Remote Administration Tools.

She dragged the big RAT over to a clock tower of rotting bricks. A white mist swirled around the base.

Our prisoners squealed so I had to shout. "What is this spooky place?"

"We can hide the RATs in the tower while you make a plan," White-Rabbit said. "The big RAT must first have new clothes. It is so embarrassing to be seen with a creature wearing torn pants."

13. I Help a Prisoner Escape

The little RAT tried to convince us that it was a good admin tool, which just happened to work remotely. "I help fix computers for a team with members located in different cities, which is why my pockets are filled with mouses."

Here is important advice about computers: Never trust a RAT unless you know who is controlling it.

Thus, we had no choice but to lock up the little RAT with the big RAT.

I yelled at the small RAT to "Shut up!" The varmint talked nonstop since we captured it.

Mouses climbed out of the smaller RAT's pockets and swarmed the cell. The mouses made matters more miserable for the big RAT.

Since we had two RATs, no telling what White-Rabbit might do to the big RAT because it was now lying on the floor dirtying its clothes. I yanked out a piece of cheese from my pocket and threw it in the cell. "I'll make sure White-Rabbit doesn't hurt you, if you promise to help me," I whispered to the big RAT.

He spoke with a rough accent, like a sewer rat. "Anything you want, girlie. Just get me away from these mouses."

White-Rabbit's last comment before she went to sleep was, "Oh, dear, the big RAT has torn the sleeve of his new shirt. Whatever shall we do with it?"

White-Rabbit might do away with the big RAT when she woke up because the RAT did not have a good fashion sense. It was freaky the way White-Rabbit slept with her eyes wide open glaring at the big RAT.

I pushed the sleeping White-Rabbit aside and entered the jail cell.

By the time White-Rabbit woke up, I was holding the big Rat's shackles.

The door clanged shut.

I stood in a corner, surrounded by mouses and two RATs. "Come on, White-Rabbit, unlock the door," I yelled in a shaky voice.

She just stared with mean eyes.

"Okay. What do you want?" I said with a big sigh.

"If the Rats get you back to your world, you must turn me into a fashion model," she said.

"I promise to find some fashion shows for avatars," I grumbled, not really into fashion video games.

"Goodbye then!" Poof! The door opened and White-Rabbit vanished.

Quick, I grabbed the big RAT and jumped out of the cell.

I slammed the door on the smaller RAT and the mouses it was in control of. "If what you say is true that you're a good RAT, then your team will restart you. At that point, you will vanish from this cell. Good luck to you," I said.

"Don't trust this human," the smaller RAT screamed at the big RAT. "She is not a team player!"

We started down a darkened hallway. The big RAT walking in front and insisting he would not try to escape if freed. "I am not a team player either," he said.

"Which is why I'm keeping you shackled," I said.

"Wait! You might need my help," the smaller RAT hollered.

I went back to the jail cell. "If you're really a good RAT, then why did you enter the computer through a hole dug by a mole? A user would have invited you in to help."

The little RAT appeared more cunning than the big RAT. Its beady eyes shifted as if it was searching for an excuse. Well, two Remote Administration Tools might be better than one.

A familiar, heart-wrenching whinny echoed from a cell near the exit of the tower. "I did not really mean to do it, Monsieur Enchanter, not really. I confess. Do not make me into a door nail!"

"Barebones?" I said and poked my face at the barred window.

The horsey security guard looked out from between the bars. The prison bars framed a stick-horse, wearing the white collar of a priest. A long, white, Louis IV type wig framed his face. Spiral curls flowed from his skull to the middle of his pipe-like body. He had tied a blue, French scarf around his nose holes and mouth. "Who goes there?" His voice was muffled by his scarf, but still understandable.

"It's me. Alicia!"

"However did you get inside the computer, mademoiselle? I do not remember; so much has happened. I am practicing my confession. The Enchanter accuses me of being a traitor. He has called for the same guillotine that beheaded the French king. There is to be a trial at four o'clock in the *City of Memory Chips*. I have put on my confessing collar. I am so sorry; I did not mean to do it," he said, wiping his eyes against the bars.

"Who exactly is the Enchanter?" I said, remembering that the brand name of the computer was *Enchanter*.

"The Enchanter is our CPU, our Central Processing Unit. Without him, we can do nothing."

"Does the Enchanter accuse you, because he thinks I hacked into the computer while you were in charge of security?" I crossed my fingers behind my back.

"Ah, you must not worry your heart out, human. They believe lightning shorted out the computer, because the PC was not plugged into a surge protector."

"The computer was not plugged into anything," I mumbled.

"I am in prison, due to the Trojan-virus. Since I am head of security, it is my fault the Trojan infected our Computer Land."

"How did this Trojan-virus get in?" I asked.

Barebones explained that a Trojan horse carried the virus.

"I'll help you escape," I squeaked.

"Ah, mademoiselle, nobody has ever escaped from the Tower," he said. Barebones pointed to a window in the hallway.

Alligator tails flopped across a water pool surrounding the tower.

"There are alligators in the moat?" I said.

"No, just their tails can be downloaded from the Chinese Internet. Alligators are fashion donors, who give their bodies to become laptop carry bags," he said.

"I'm so very sorry."

"Why are you sorry? It is the alligators' wish to be fashionable. Do not weep for the alligators. Their bags are dyed in many colors."

"I am extremely sorry for you, Barebones."

"Do not feel so guilty," he said.

My mouth dropped open. "Then, you know that it was I who..."

"Yes, you let the Trojan-virus loose," Barebones said.

The big RAT ground its teeth, a sign that it was happy at the news that I released the virus. Therefore, I said no more about my remorse.

Barebones could not see the RATs standing by the door. The stick-horse cocked his skull in a curious manner. "Your eyes are watering, mademoiselle. I am programmed with little memory and a list of instructions, whereas you are still human with a heart and a brain."

"There is longing in your voice, Barebones."

"Impossible! Alicia, be careful or the virus will strike you, too. Cover your face for protection against the virus." He untied the scarf from his mouth and threw the scarf at me. "What happened to your teeth hardware?"

"I lost my braces," I said, picking up the scarf.

"Be careful then, so you do not fall. Au revoir, until we meet again."

The stick-horse hopped away from the window.

The key to the RATs cell worked on the lock of Barebone's prison door. "I can't let the Enchanter delete you, because of me. Come with us."

"Us?" Barebones said.

Both RATs stuck their heads in the cell.

"Eek! What are you doing with RATs? I'd rather take my chances with the Enchanter," Barebones said.

"Don't be stupid," I said and pushed the stick-horse from his jail cell.

The big RAT snapped its teeth at him and laughed at the shaking stick-horse.

"Some security," the small RAT snorted.

"No wonder you got a Trojan-virus into the computer, Boss," the big RAT said with deep admiration.

"Yeah," I said in a tough sounding voice. I needed the big RAT to think I was a criminal.

As soon as we left the tower, Barebones insisted on going his own way. "They'll be looking for me. I have no wish to endanger you, mademoiselle," he said.

"My face is on a milk carton," I said.

The big RAT bowed. "My hero," it said and lowered its back so that I could ride it.

The stick-horse ran in one direction. I rode the RAT in the other direction. The small RAT led the way. There was no longer a need for shackles for either RAT. Both RATs pledged to obey me.

I gained the big RAT's respect because it believed I was trying to destroy the computer. I had to go along and pretend to be a cracker who needed help from my brother, a pirate, in order to annihilate everything.

"Including us?" the big RAT said with a wide grin.

The big RAT was obviously crazy. As for the small RAT, as soon as it discovered from Barebones that I was a user, it dropped the three mouses hidden in its pockets and swore allegiance to me.

Two RATs were now under my control. With any luck, the RATs could help me escape back to my world.

According to Barebones, the Trojan-virus could destroy everything in the computer, including me, a virtual human girl.

14. I Hang from a DVD Drive

The big RAT ran its programming code and took control of the computer camera. The Rat removed a bag tied to a cane. It then held the cane up, and I looked through the handle and was able to see the study.

The door lay on the carpet, its hinges dangling from the doorframe. There was no sign of Axel.

The north study wall was thumb tacked with Arthur's posters of vampires, monster trucks, and football schedules.

Rotating the cane allowed me to see the entire study. My posters of Math tables and greatest movie quotes hung on the south study wall.

On the ceiling were glow-in-the-dark stars and planets.

In the family digital picture hanging on the east wall, Dad seemed to snap his suspenders, his moustache vibrating with displeasure.

Mom's belly shook with shock, her hair standing on end.

Axel glared with different colored eyes making him look cross-eyed. Axel was born with a brown eye and a green eye. My brother was proud of his oddity and refused to wear contact lenses to correct his eye coloring.

Axel's thin face seemed to grow bigger in the family picture, while my eyebrow in the photo arched higher. Axel was six inches taller and muscular. He had hogged the camera that day. The photographer snapped only my left eye and brow.

Unfortunately, no one was in the study.

A crack of light shone above me.

"There's a way out! You must take me to the top," I told the big RAT.

"You should know, Boss, that a RAT is a better swimmer than climber," it said.

"Fine! I will go by myself. Turn on the speakers and the microphone. Both of you wait here."

The RATs nodded their heads.

I shoved the *Irresponsible Alicia* file-folder between my teeth. I pulled myself up wires, hanging like branches from the walls and inched toward the light.

The plastic ledge was slippery. I stretched my fingers to a slit from where the light shone, but the opening was too high.

Screws in the wall were useful like mountain climber's tools. Huffing and puffing, I heaved myself up to the next screw, climbing from one screw to the other, and another.

I hauled myself up to the last screw near where the light shone through.

I grabbed onto the ledge, lifting my leg up.

I peeked through the slit into the study.

I was on the DVD drive! A girl, narrower than a DVD, should be able to exit through this opening.

I began to squeeze my way through the slit.

Suddenly, a DVD popped in.

I pushed against the DVD. "Axel, do not put the DVD in the drive!" I shouted.

The big RAT had turned the microphone on because I heard my brother mutter, "The DVD is sticking in the drive. Darn computer is making that buzzing noise again."

The buzzing noise was I. The RAT had turned the speakers on, but Axel could not hear my words because I was tiny.

"Axel! It's Alicia," I yelled with all my might.

Jeez, now my voice sounded like crackling electricity through the speakers.

There was a click and Axel turned off the speakers.

The DVD clicked into place, spinning me on the disk.

Axel said, "Letters have been left on the screen." He read the message:

> !qləH—nɿəɔnoɔ yɒm ʇi moʜw oT
> ƨu bəqqɒnbiʞ ƨəmonϙ ɿəʇuqmoƆ
> .ʇluɒʇ ym ʇon ƨi ʇI
> ɒiɔilA .wobniw ybuʇƨ əʜʇ ʞɒəɿd ʇon bib I

"What the heck does that mean?"

Eek! I mistakenly left a mirror message. Instead, the message should have been written backwards. The message on the monitor screen in red lipstick had been understandable to me. For Axel *in front* of the monitor, the words would show backwards to him. Axel would have to put a mirror up to the message to read it correctly.

"The screen needs to be refreshed," Axel said.

"No, Axel! Use a mirror," I cried out but my voice sounded like hiccups in the speakers.

"The gibberish is erased now. No harm done," he said. "Mm, Dad's email tool is open."

My heart beat excitedly, knowing Axel had no qualms about reading Dad's email.

"Darn, the mail server is down," he said.

The DVD shook, rattling me on the disk.

The DVD whirled so fast, my head spun. As data bytes transferred from the DVD to the memory of the computer, I slid across the disk, my legs zipping like scissors.

I lost my balance and flew off the DVD.

Quick, I grabbed onto the edge of the DVD and hung on for dear life. My legs dangled in the air as the disk spun.

Far below, the big RAT lumbered away, deserting me. The big RAT must have thought I was done for and took its cane and thus, the ability to look through the camera. Hopefully, the big RAT turned the speakers back on and left the microphone on. If only I could communicate with Axel!

At least the small RAT was still here, proving it really was a good Remote Administration Tool and a team player.

My fingernails were losing their grip on the DVD.

15. A Pirate Comes to My Rescue

I yelled down at the RAT to, "Get me back on the DVD."

In a millisecond, I was back on the DVD, spinning like on a lightning-fast merry-go-round. With the RAT's help, I was stable. The spinning disk did not throw me off.

My only chance now of speaking to Axel was to play the DVD game with him.

With the aid of the small RAT, I became a player in the video game. There is a cool side effect of being a cast member of a video game DVD. While spinning dizzily on the disk, I also stood in a desert background of a video game. What an experience! It was awesome being in two places at once, the DVD, and the monitor. My reflection was in the mirrored closet, behind Axel. Once again, I looked scared yet I gripped a spinning disk, screaming with joy.

It was nerve-wracking that Axel pirated a new game named *The Wrath of the Gnome King*. The game was in *beta mode*, so not yet ready for public release. Axel was impatient so stole a copy. Oops! I mean Axel pirated a copy. Axel claims there is a difference since he never sells the merchandise he pirates from the Internet.

Dust blew about desert scenery, with eerie, howling noises. Barefoot gnomes with long noses littered the desert. The gnomes held knives, spoons, and other cutlery as weapons. The gnomes froze in place, but those beasties can be tricky.

In the center of the game was a golden crown sticking out of the middle of a rusted boulder, from which volcanic magma flowed. In the far background were skinny, black trees, looking like a fire had rushed through the forest.

A pirate ship rocked on an ocean. The game had three terrains all mixed together with three suns.

The game was not virtual reality so the volcano was not warm. Axel sat on the study chair, gawking at me standing on top of the rusted boulder. My brother was so flabbergasted; his green eye darkened and matched his brown eye better. His face flushed an angry red. “Alicia, what are you doing playing my video game, *The Wrath of the Gnome King*? This is not a

Multi-User Edition," he said then mumbled, "What am I doing talking to an animated GIF?"

"I am not a GIF," I answered.

Axel leaned back in the armless chair, with his arms folded across his chest and an amused look on his face.

Being in two places at once was new to me. I sweated from three suns, making me feel like I was melting. My face was green from spinning on the disk, and my stomach retched. Moreover, I feared Axel could still not hear me. "Help! I really am inside the computer! This is no game, Axel!"

His face grew bigger as he thrust his head at the monitor screen. "The GIF has my bratty sister's attitude," he grumbled.

"It's because this is really me. I've become a virtual girl, Axel."

"Well, you are in such big trouble, for cracking the monitor," he said, laughing and clearly not believing in me.

"It's just a hairline crack; the bump on my head was bigger. You should be in trouble, for pirating your video game, plus the music you're playing, which I know you didn't pay for."

"I only download copyrighted stuff for myself. I don't distribute," he muttered, frowning. There was doubt in his eyes now that perhaps I was telling the truth about being inside the computer.

"You're still a thieving pirate." I pointed to a copy of *Pirate Magazine,* which lay on his lap. His black t-shirt had an iron-on picture of a green-faced monitor, wearing an eye patch, and a pirate hat with a skull and bones insignia. A wooden leg with a hook was shoved through the picture of the monitor. It looked like the hook was the left ear, and the wooden peg the right ear. Printed on the t-shirt was his tattooed avatar — Bulldog.

Axel rubbed his chest, running his hand down the computer pirate emblem on his shirt. He cleared his throat. "Well, since you're the infamous White-Rabbit, we've both joined the dark side of computing."

"I'm a hacker who breaks into computers, and does not burglarize them. I follow the ethics of the Chaos Computing Club. I simply like the challenge."

"Well, we still work in stealth and play a role in the computer underground. Look how you hacked into my video game."

"Computer-gnomes shrunk me and kidnapped me," I said.

Axel turned pale as a ghost. "Wait one minute! You are an avatar in my video game and you are talking to me like a person! What happened to the chair-arms?" he said suspiciously.

"Well, one is on the study floor, as you well know." I picked up the shrunken chair-arm that was on the floor of the monitor and held the chair-arm up to him. "I tried to hold onto the chair, but the gnomes got me," I said with a trembling lip. "The gnomes used my shoestring to haul me to the camera after shrinking me with magic." I lifted my shoe that was missing a shoestring.

He mumbled, "There was a shoestring hanging from the monitor."

I wept uncontrollably. I never cried in front of my family. My tears, along with the evidence of my abduction, convinced Axel I was telling the truth.

He grabbed the mouse and started clicking and sliding it across the mouse pad. "I wondered how you simply vanished. The window is broken. I figured you got scared when I broke down the door. Alicia! What did you do with the mouse? It doesn't work!"

"Dormouse hacked in and erased the mouse driver."

Axel clicked on the keyboard using the arrow keys. He tried multiple combinations to download a new mouse driver, access the computer register keys, execute system files, etc. He tried to bring up the Trash folder to search for the deleted mouse driver. He plugged in another mouse. Nothing worked. Everything was still frozen except for me.

Axel frantically flipped through a game manual, throwing it on the floor in disgust. He grabbed the monitor sides. "Alicia, I just installed this game. I transferred the game files to the hard disk earlier. The game advertised magical bonus features, on invisible DVD tracks. I thought this sounded cool, but the gnomes have taken control of the computer."

"Well, you're the gamer. Do something!"

"I have no experience with this game. I don't even know the rules."

Even though Axel had not clicked the game *Start* button, the gnomes began to thaw from their locked positions, sounding like cracking ice.

I screamed, ducking my head, as stalagmites and stalactites hurled at me like swords.

Axel had only added two pirates to his crew so far and his own bulldog avatar.

Odd, Axel's voice echoed from behind, saying these words, "Hey, kid sister!"

The doppelganger-side-effect of video games, which can infect a player, is a rare phenomenon. Axel's miniature double was inside the computer, waving from behind. He jumped up and down by the wires and monitor guts, while at the same time, the human Axel sat in the study, in the real world. However, Axel's doppelganger was not his mere reflection, nor was Axle controlling him. The doppelganger had a brain. The pint-sized Axel danced inside the monitor, whistling and singing, happy to have materialized. The only other difference between the two Axels was their switched eyes. The real Axel had a right green eye and a left brown eye. His mirror image, the cyber Axel, had a right brown eye and a left green eye.

"This is not good," Axel said in the study.

Axel pushed the DVD eject button.

The magic DVD would not eject.

16. The Wrath of the Gnome King

Gnomes gnashed their teeth. One gnome carried a net to capture me.

Axel's pirate avatar, Bulldog, and the other two pirates bravely fought the gnomes off.

Bulldog growled and bit the gnomes. Unfortunately, Axel had not yet chosen a weapon for his avatar when the gnomes attacked. Bulldog and the pirates were soon outnumbered.

The pirates vanished from the game, leaving behind a sword and flag with skull and crossbones.

"The game is buggy," Axel said and sounded frustrated.

Gnomes chased me. "Do you think the game is buggy, Sherlock?" I yelled at Axel. "What with a giant bug walking around like it owns the game!" I circled the volcano.

"Come back here! Don't you get smart with me," Axel said.

I came back around the volcano. "Well one of us has to be smart! You're so dumb playing a pirated game filled with gnomes," I shouted.

"Well I'm not the idiot trapped inside the computer," he yelled back. "Oh, blasted! Here they come! If only I could man the pirate ship."

The abandoned ship rocked on an oasis in the middle of a desert. A large palm tree growing from sand shaded the ship.

"It's the bug that has the game confused," I said.

Axel's mini double sweated. He was dressed for warmth with a high-necked shirt and jacket. My brother's doppelganger clearly did not wish to fight. He stood on the pirate ship with his hands on his hips. Axel's double began a long, lengthy speech about making peace.

"Too bad your doppelganger is a chicken," I said to Axel.

A gnome hit me on the head with a giant ladle. She looked like my grandma, but I punched her nose anyway.

Mini-Axel, the doppelganger, was definitely my brother. "I'll help you, Alicia," the mini said.

He grabbed a rope, hanging from the pirate ship. Mini-Axel swung to the boulder.

He steadied his rocky feet, before letting the rope go. He yanked the sword from the stone, raising it in victory.

The virtual Axel stood, with his knees bent, and his sword pointed at the gnomes. I had never been so proud of my brother, even if he was just his doppelganger.

He whirled the sword around, knocking off some gnomes' heads.

The other gnomes ran towards mini-Axel. They climbed the boulder, slipping, sliding, and snarling.

Gnomes stood on each other's shoulders, forming a gnome-ladder to the top of the rock.

I hid behind a cactus.

There was a sound of trumpets, followed by dancing fairies. The Gnome King marched in front of the procession. The Gnome King was the tallest of the gnomes. The king was, also, the ugliest. He had a big, crooked nose, long pointy ears, and teeth like a picket fence.

A brown bug crawled in front of the king. The bug was so enormous its antennae looked more like horns. The bug poked its antennae at Axel's doppelganger.

Gnomes captured mini-Axel and dragged him before their king.

The Gnome King pointed a long finger at the doppelganger, demanding to know, "Where is your sister?"

Given that, the doppelganger tried to rescue me and risked his own freedom, I now thought of him as I would the real Axel. *I must free Axel,* I thought.

It was as if my other brother, the Axel sitting in the study all safe and sound, could hear my thoughts. He shook his head and mouthed the words, *you better not, Alicia.* He pointed at a hag dressed in white, walking towards the king and his ragtag court of gnomes and worshipful fairies.

It was the W-W-W, the infamous Wicked-Witch-West! The witch was short and mean looking. She had buggy eyes and a long sharp nose that grew from the top of her forehead. She was dressed in rags that swept her feet. The witch had bad teeth.

The witch had her own followers, some of the Oz hackers. The hackers looked in terrible shape. The witch had clearly taken her fury out on them because their hacking skills were not good enough to find the pot of gold at the end of the rainbow.

"Alicia is the latest technology and no one had claimed the virtual human," the witch said.

My heart beat fearfully. *What did the witch mean that no one had claimed me? Had, like in past tense!*

With her huge nostrils, the witch had a nose for money. She sniffed a piece of paper and sighed with rapture. "I have just come from the Internet and the United States Patent and Trademark office," she said, waving the paper. "I have registered a patent on Alicia. The technology of virtual humans now belongs to me." Alicia is more valuable than a pot of gold at the end of the rainbow."

My knees shook at the thought of being enslaved to the Wicked-Witch-West like the Oz hackers. The witch beat up Tin-Man for not finding the pot of gold. She beheaded Scarecrow. Now, she claimed to own me simply because she filed a piece of paper with the U.S. Patent office on my technology.

"Surrender your sister," the witch said to Axel. "I must take Alicia apart and see how she works."

I was so scared at the thought of belonging to the witch, that I fell off the spinning DVD.

17. I Fall Down a Computer Hole

I screamed, falling down a dark hole.

"Alicia!" the two Axels hollered, followed by eerie silence. The speakers must have turned off.

Clouds crammed with pictures and thoughts resembling comic strips, whizzed by. I must have fallen into the computer's memory banks.

Suddenly, a light flashed. There was a whirling noise, and a rug shot out of a circuit board.

The flying carpet kept trying to get under me.

I struggled to stay away from the rug, thinking it belonged to the witch. There was also the fact that we had been playing the buggy *Wrath of the Gnome King* in a desert. Advanced-desert transport was not to be trusted. This mode of transportation is rare. Nowadays, flying carpets are found only at *The Museum of Carpets and World of Flying Carpets* display.

Memory chips were below with sharp pins sticking up that looked painful to fall on them. There was no choice but to swing my legs onto the flying carpet, to avoid falling into a pit of thorny hardware.

In a déjà vu moment, I flew through the Java party's flowered archway.

The flying carpet landed on what was left of the picnic table.

The carpet flipped, depositing me on a serving plate. Ouch! My ankle was twisted.

The carpet stuffed an apple in my mouth and then wrapped my nose and mouth with the scarf Barebones had given me. It then tied me up like a trussed turkey. The carpet transformed into a checkered tablecloth, sliding beneath me.

A dinner bell went ting-a-ling.

Okay, now I am really in for it. The witch plans to carve me like a turkey to see what my technology is made of.

I could not scream for help, due to the apple in my mouth. Anyway, my only companion was Oxy-Moron. His flat head lay on the ground. "The silence is deafening. Thank you for calling and have a nice day," Oxy-Moron said in his Indian accent.

I bit into the apple, planning to eat my way out of my predicament.

A small, jeweled crown and bare foot stuck out from the side of a Java cup. A hoe and spade leaned against the cup, along with a treasure bag pile.

"The Gnome King," I mumbled with a mouth full of apple bits. The king cleverly disguised himself as a garden gnome, perhaps to fool the witch.

He stepped from his hiding place. The king untied me and removed the apple from my mouth.

"Thanks, your Majesty," I said and quickly rewrapped my face with the scarf for protection against the virus that attacked the Java party. Green slime was everywhere so I tightened the scarf. Since I was flat, like a paper doll, the sides of my head touched, giving me a wallop of a headache.

The king was pleased I recognized him.

"It's because you are uglier than the other gnomes," I said, without thinking.

He stood with his fists on his hips, thanking me for gloriously insulting him, as only a ruler should be. He snapped his finger, transforming his garden rags into royal blue, fur-lined clothes. Gnomes tend to be antisocial and rarely speak even to each other, yet here was the King of the Gnomes, smiling while he puffed on a backward-S pipe.

Suddenly, he lifted his scepter above my head, as if he would stab my throat. "I have been watching you, User, for some time," he said with a thick, German accent. "As Gnome King, I cannot take credit for something we did not do. It was you, Alicia, who broke the computer, not us. You must take credit for this, accept awards, make speeches, and all other honor that comes when you have done a good job. You must not give credit for your escapades to the White-Rabbit, but should use your own name."

"And you should admit to being stupid. You cannot even spell. The email you sent read, *We no who u r. We have been watching u,*" I said.

"I don't need a spell checker to spell *delete with wiping*. The Enchanter will ensure you are forever erased and cannot be recycled from the trash. I shall turn you in and claim the reward of becoming a desktop icon. You are sweating, Cracker, and you are trembling," he said.

"I am not a cracker. You know, darn well, your gnomes kidnapped me!"

He licked his finger, running his digit down my cheek. He stuck his finger in his mouth. "You taste salty, which proves you are a cracker."

"Tears are salty, stupid! The White-Rabbit is a celebrated hacker," I said, shivering at the saliva he left on my skin.

"Do not get upset. The Enchanter would not delete a bunny, or a cracker," he said.

"Why, then, is the Enchanter after me?"

"The Enchanter put your name on a milk carton because you were last seen with the Trojan horse. In the horse's belly was the virus that is infecting the computer's health. The 21st Century is the dawn of the healthy computer. If there had been Trojan-virus, worm-flu, piggy-backers, or other illness last century, it would not have mattered. Health-nutty, energy-saving CPUs even do yoga now. When you think the computer is running slow, or stuck, and you click and bang-bang your mouse, it is the Enchanter, meditating, floating above memory chips with his knees open, and sitting in his yoga pose to slim down on power."

"I won't take credit for the Trojan-virus. Your Trojan-gnomes directed the fleas," I said.

"It is a computer-gnome's nature to direct chaos," he said, shrugging his shoulders. "It is in your nature to give credit to others. Do not be so modest about your abilities."

The king took a bite out of a sheet of paper that looked awful familiar. "That's my..." I said.

"Yes, your English essay tastes scrumptious, Alicia, especially the lies and tall tales. I must live up to the crime of which you have accused me. I have a reputation to uphold," he said and swallowed. "Verbs are my favorite and are zesty. Pronouns taste sour, except for *me, myself,* and *I,* which have a more selfish flavor. Nouns make me spit up. As for numbers, numerals constipate me, especially the number 2. Adjectives are a delicacy. The healthiest words to eat are cuss words. Cussing is comfort food."

He grabbed another paper. "My second course, your history lesson," he said.

History? I was forgetting something important, but what? *Think, Alicia! Think!*

The gnome, who had stood on top of the camera, had asked me to say sorry. He then kidnapped me when I did not apologize. "I'm sorry; I gave the gnomes credit for breaking Dad's old computer. I apologize for blaming you for eating my homework," I now blurted out.

"Too late for sorry," the King said.

Think, Alicia! There had been a Java party earlier, but there was no one here now except the Gnome King, Cuckoo, and me. The spelling bee hung passed out over an empty Java cup. His wing was drooped over the cup.

Suddenly, the bee's stinger stuck straight up in the air, and then pointed to the corner. The bee was too drunk on Java to spell, but was trying to confide something.

The king walked over to the *Java Virtual Machine*. He flipped up the nozzle, and slid beneath it with his mouth open. No drops of Java fell on his tongue. He shoved his fist through the empty machine.

Eureka! I knew what Cuckoo was trying to say. Java programmed a game as magical as the Wrath of the Gnome King. This meant the king must have more Java to increase his supernatural powers.

Cuckoo must have watched me hide a pot of Java and now pointed to where it was, reminding me. I inched my way to the foot of the table where the Java was hidden.

I shoved the pot under the king's nose. "Would you like a cup, your majesty," I said with a sweet smile.

He held an empty cup, the cup rattling against the saucer. "Kind acts do not change things between us, virtual human. You are too valuable. I must turn you in and win that reward so my desktop icon will be undeletable. I shall become more powerful and at last, overthrow the Enchanter. I will become Emperor of Computer Land," he said.

I threw the Java pot at his face.

The king dropped to his knees.

I hobbled toward the flowered archway.

The king sucked the Java from his royal robe. He then swept the ground with his tongue.

"Where's my army? Go after her, numbskulls! Do I have to do everything myself?" the king screamed. "March! March!"

Gnomes popped up from nowhere, littering the garden.

They danced in lines, fluttering their legs like Irish stepdancers.

A chair popped down from a rope hanging from a buzzing helicopter.

Axel's doppelganger grinned down at me. He wore sunglasses and a pilot's uniform.

I sat on the chair, and he lifted me into the chopper.

"Axel, you read the game manual!" I hugged my brother's doppelganger. My arms went right through his body.

"I'm unstable," Axel said. He waved about as if a shotgun blasted him. He let off electrical sparks.

"Oh, Axel, you don't look well," I said.

He was bald and his nose smashed into his face, which was a grayish color. His brown eye was missing.

"I barely survived playing level 1. This is level 2," he said, groaning.

"What can I do to help?" I said, panicking.

"I'm low on memory," he said.

Axel concentrated on flying the helicopter through a cyber forest of rainbow-colored trees.

His head hit the bubble windshield, with a loud crack.

The helicopter spun, crashing into the woods.

18. Ever Been Burned into a Screen?

I limped from the burning helicopter while pulling Axel from the wreckage.

What was left of my brother's doppelganger was a mess of wires. Nevertheless, I counted, "One, two. Come on, Axel! Restart the game! Please! You've got to advance to level 3."

He fluttered his eyelashes, pulling weakly at my hand. "I came to warn you," he whispered. He shifted his eyes to the right, his body stiffening.

I turned my head to what he was looking at, expecting gnomes to litter the forest, but instead…

"Quick! Look away!" Axel said.

"It's me. She's a clone," I whispered. "How did I duplicate?"

"Your doppelganger, also, transferred to the DVD when you played the game," he said.

The pirated game had been magical and buggy. Axel's doppelganger materialized when he played the game while in the study. I had been on the DVD spinning with the video game. It was logical that I, too, fell victim to the video game doppelganger-side-effect.

It took most of Axel's strength to speak. "Never stare at the other Alicia's eyes. To lock eyes with your own doppelganger is a death omen," he said, panting.

"No, Axel, the other Alicia is just bad luck, like you are. To see a relative's doppelganger is a sign of danger or bad luck," I said, hastily. Yet, having my doppelganger, looking over my shoulder and breathing into my ear, creeped me out.

"I can't hold on much longer. I'm sorry to let you down, little sister," Axel said in a weak voice.

"Oh, Axel, you never let me down. You saved me from the Gnome King. I did not mean it about bad luck. You're my brother, my good luck charm." I tried to grasp his hand, but my hand went right through his. "Stay with me, Axel, please! Don't leave me!"

He shivered and an odd sensation tingled up my arm. The sparks he let off were like glowing cinders. Axel felt like ashes yet, I could feel the grass beneath his ghostly hand.

Slowly…Axel faded.

"No!" I felt like I was drowning. "Axel, no! Axel!"

"Alicia, I'm still here."

"Axel?" His voice came from behind.

Axel was trapped inside a block of ice. He let out a deep sigh and then a devastating silence. He had become screen burn-in. When a non-moving image is left in place for too long on a monitor, the image might be burned into the monitor screen. The image would resemble a ghost of the original.

That darn buggy game! I pounded the ice, pushing and shoving from the outside, but could not cause even a crack in the cube.

My own doppelganger had disappeared.

I fell back and laid flat on the grass. I cried myself to sleep.

19. A Ghost Haunts Me

The slightest wisp of movement woke me.

"Axel?" I said, turning my head to the large ice cube.

The ice had melted. My brother's doppelganger was gone.

My own doppelganger was lying down and hugging me.

I screamed and twisted my head to avoid my doppelganger's eyes. Quick, I snatched my file from the ground and ran.

Branches scratched my arms, yet I stumbled deeper into the woods.

Someone breathed heavily.

I breathed out.

Someone breathed in.

Branches reached out.

I screamed, moving faster.

Something brushed against my cheek.

I waved my arms, but nothing was there.

Someone or something pushed against my back.

I limped toward a spot of light, shaped like a teardrop.

I stopped and hugged my hands to my hurting sides.

A swarm of ghostly images flew past.

I flung my arms out and covered my head.

"Alicia," a muffled voice said.

I felt goose bumps on my arms. "Show yourself then and quit acting so scary. Do not be offended when I don't look at you," I said, thinking it must be my doppelganger.

My stalker stepped from behind a tree and held up his palms. "It's me. Axel," he said and sounded like he was speaking with cotton in his mouth.

"Oh, Axel, I'm so happy to see you," I said, shivering with fear. Once again, my brother's doppelganger transformed into something else. "However did you escape?"

"I graduated to level 3 in the video game."

My brother was still trying to save me. Axel was still working in the study wracking his brain on a plan of rescue.

"But I can see right through you," I said.

"I know," he said with a deep sigh. "I've turned into a ghost."

He is no longer Axel's doppelganger but his ghost image, I thought. Ghosting is normally done to create a clone for backup and restore purposes.

"Something is very wrong with the computer, Alicia. I have tried everything to stop the video game and restart. The computer is running without electricity. Even weirder, the battery power backup, the UPS, is dead."

"You pirated a game containing gnome magic, so I'm not surprised."

"With my upgraded game level, I should have reverted back to my doppelganger self but instead, I'm even more unstable."

"You are Axel's ghost image and therefore, a clone of my brother."

"I'm a ghost."

"You should not be unstable."

"I'm actually a fragment, left behind by level 2. Consequently, I may vanish at any moment. Thinking about my unstableness makes me jittery." He wiggled about like snow on a television screen.

"Your condition might be caused by the virus," I said.

"My computer has a virus?"

"You mean *our* computer has a virus."

"Alicia! You didn't!"

"Of course not," I said, crossing my fingers behind my back.

"Why is the Gnome King after you then?" he said suspiciously.

"No reason," I squeaked.

"Alicia," he said in his big brother, scolding tone.

I stamped my foot. "Oh, alright, the Gnome King tricked me and I let in a virus. I did not do anything wrong."

"Right! So this mess is *not* your fault," he said, giving me a familiar look.

The darkening sky caused my knees to knock together. "We must find a way out," I said, changing the subject. I flung away the folder labeled *Irresponsible Alicia.*

"What was that you just threw?" he said.

"Nothing. A lesson learned."

"According to the game manual, I think, an opening is this way," he said.

If Axel's doppelganger was unstable, maybe he was not trustworthy. "You think an opening is this way? You don't know for sure?" I said.

Suddenly, something shoved my shoulder, pushing me to my knees.

My doppelganger ran away, laughing wickedly.

Axel held out a hand to help me rise.

I grabbed at his ghostly hand, shivering at a cold, fog sensation. My hand went right through him. I bit my lip, holding back my tears.

"Alicia, I know you're a good person and mean well. This time, it really is not your fault that your doppelganger is black hearted, like an evil twin," he said.

I wailed because everything went dark. "Axel?"

"Shush, don't cry. Your brother…I must be rebooting."

"Or maybe the computer is dying from the virus. Even though you're just a ghost image, I'm sorry to bring this mess on you."

The lights went on and Axel smiled. "You're growing up, Alicia. Your last thoughts are of me and not yourself."

"I am unsure I ever want to grow up. Growing up hurts too much," I mumbled.

Presto! At these words, an old childhood friend hopped in front of us. My old avatar, March-Hare, blocked our way. "I've been waiting for you nearly two years, Alicia," she said.

20. Mad as a March Hare

I began hacking at the age of seven on a cold spring day in March. The avatar I chose for my handle then was March-Hare.

"I've missed you," I said to March-Hare and bent to kiss the bunny's nose.

March-Hare moved her head, poking me in the eye with a long ear. Like most hares, March-Hare was shy.

"This is my brother," I said.

"I remember Axel," March-Hare grumbled. "I see you've turned another member of your family into a ghost."

"I've never turned anyone into a ghost. It's not my fault that Axel is ghostly."

"Nothing is ever your fault, Alicia. Since you abandoned your childhood, I would have thought by now you would be mature," March-Hare said.

"I am grown up," I said.

March-Hare made a face.

"Do you know the way out?" I said.

She hopped around and wiggled her tail. "I'll help lead you out."

"Come on, Axel," I said excitedly.

"March-Hare doesn't seem to like me," my brother said.

"March-Hare was always jealous. We didn't part on good terms."

"Well, what's going to happen to me when you leave?" Axel said.

"Isn't it kind of cool being a ghost?"

"I could pirate the internet more easily."

I rolled my eyes. Pirating was all Axel ever thought about, even his doppelganger.

We followed March-Hare out of the forest and into a clearing.

March-Hare hopped around. "Here we are!"

I turned in a circle. "We're still in the guts of the computer. There is no door or any way out."

"You never said you wanted to get out of the computer. I assumed you referred to the forest. You should say what you mean," March-Hare said.

"Well, I mean what I say, which is the same thing."

"Then you might as well say you want the computer to get out of you," March-Hare said.

"Oh, you're confusing!"

"Here, have some wine." March-Hare handed me an empty glass.

I held the glass out and waited. "Where is the wine?"

"There isn't any wine," March-Hare said.

"Then it wasn't very civil of you to offer wine," I said angrily.

"Then it wasn't very civil of you to abandon me when you left elementary school." March-Hare boxed my nose.

"You're mad," I said.

"Furiously heartless," March-Hare said, hopping continuously.

"I meant that you're crazy."

"I meant that you broke my heart, Alicia. After nearly four years together, you deserted me Easter before enrolling in Middle School!"

"I grew up and needed an avatar who reflected more of who I had become."

"You mean not a fat, short bunny!"

"You mean cute baby fat," I said.

"A ton of lard," March-Hare said.

"A ton is 2,000 pounds. You don't weigh a ton."

"I only eat carrots but still gain weight. It took a year to feel better about myself after you left."

"I'm happy for you, March-Hare. You don't seem as neurotic."

"I turned to the church and found religion, like the Easter Hare," she said.

"You mean, the Easter Bunny."

"There you go again, making me feel bad because I'm not a rabbit but a hare. Just when I was beginning to feel good about myself again, you rain on my Easter parade."

March-Hare pushed her glasses up and straightened her tie. She cleared her throat and recited: "When I was a child, I used to speak like a child, think like a child, reason like a child; when I became a middle-school hacker, I did away with childish things, such as my bunny."

"That's sort of from the Bible," I said.

"The verse is from the book of Corinthians, Chapter 13, verse 11. A copy of the Bible is in the archives. The Enchanter freed me from the archives where you dumped me. I am saved, Alicia. Can you say the same about yourself, if the virus destroys Computer Land?"

March-Hare hopped away.

"Wait," I yelled. "Why did the Enchanter free you? What did you give him in return?"

"The Enchanter rewarded me with my own desktop icon," she shouted.

"You Judas," I yelled at March-Hare's back.

21. His Most Magical Enchanter

Members of Brute Force Blocking Software surrounded the other Axel and me.

Grim Reaper grabbed me around the waist. "The Enchanter demands to see you," she mumbled.

"I won't leave you. Stay strong," Axel said.

The virus had struck *Cyber City*. Green-slime covered about a third of the city. Neon lights wiggled on broken pavement, cloaking the city in semi-darkness. Hardware lay crushed beneath fallen windows. Most of the bright lights were out, and the fan no longer blew a warm breeze. Thus, frost engulfed the windows that were undamaged. Icicles hung from the window frames.

Human-like creatures burned software piles and huddled around the flames, trying to keep warm.

Shadowy figures stood in the fires' fringes, waving their arms about to fan the heat, like mock turtles swimming in the sea. Most of the cyber shadows were too weak to be threatening and sighed in melancholy voices.

"If the anti-virus was useless against the Trojan, even we could get infected, like these shadows," Axel said, gulping.

"Perhaps humans and ghosts are immune to the virus," I said.

Grim Reaper pinched me to silence me.

"Maybe my brother and I are infected," I loudly said.

Grim Reaper ignored us.

My stomach was queasy. Perhaps it was the virus.

"I...your human brother, may be able to manually remove the virus, but he must first discover that the computer is infected," Axel whispered.

"But as his doppelganger, you are Axel, though he sits in the study playing *The Wrath of the Gnome King* or whatever. Can you tell my brother about the virus?" I whispered back.

"We have our own minds, though I share his memories. His order was to steal the helicopter. Once the helicopter was shot down, Axel no longer has a clue about my thoughts or actions."

"Thank goodness, a Trojan does not make copies of itself, like some viruses so it spreads slower. By now, maybe Axel has figured out that the computer has a virus," I said.

"A Trojan virus has the power to delete," he said, his voice sounding bleak. "Sometimes, the easiest solution to fix a Trojan is to erase everything and reinstall."

"Oh," I said, feeling faint. "Surely Axel would realize that he would be erasing me."

"If a backup of the computer was made, after you were kidnapped by the gnomes, you could be restored from the backup; else you will just vanish," he said.

"I doubt there is a backup of the computer that recent. Axel will permanently erase me if he reinstalls," I said. "You might return when Axel plays a video game again, but I..."

Grim Reaper ripped off my scarf and snarled. "The virus deletes programs. Data vanishes. Programs crash into buildings and woodlands. Just look at what's happened to the city!"

"The virus is not my fault. It was the beasties!" I yelled.

Axel shouted. "Protect my sister from the virus. Give her back the scarf."

"Alicia does not need protection, since she is human," Grim Reaper said.

"Don't believe her," Axel whispered. "The virus was created by a human, so you may catch it. Your race is creative, but also destructive. Maybe a portal of escape is nearby."

"If we could just get away from Grim Reaper," I said, sighing.

A flashing sign floated above the golden doors to the *Arena of Memory Chips.* The sign read, *Entertainment Today. Escape Feats, Card Games, Hat Tricks, Memory Pranks, Money Cons, Illusions, Supernaturals, and Executions. All conjured up by the Enchanter. All magic performed before a live audience, with no added visual effects.*

Grim Reaper shoved me through the door, and it closed behind us with a bang.

The circular arena was made of smoke and mirrors. In the center was a giant computer chip with sizzling circuits.

"That must be the Enchanter," Axel said. He pointed to a man-like creature dangling from the air above the computer chip. The Enchanter was the brains of the computer. His black, wavy hair was parted in the middle.

A strait jacket bound the Enchanter's arms with the sleeves buckled to his back. A chain bound his ankles, wrapped around his chest, and locked at the middle of his back.

The Enchanter hung upside down, so it was a wonder his blue tailcoat stayed in place. Even more amazing—a purple top hat balanced on his head.

The Enchanter emitted electrical streaks from his veins and his skin stunk of burning wires. Smoke rings rose from his head. His clothes gave an occasional zap because the threads were electronic. He had a long, pointy-head, shaped like a volcanic brain.

Chairs floated in the air.

I chased a chair and caught one.

Axel, being a ghost, hung in the air.

The giant, grey computer chip stretched high up, appearing bottomless at the other end.

It was eerily silent while the Enchanter swung in the air.

"What's he doing?" I whispered.

Popcorn kernels flew from every direction.

"Sh, he's solving the virus," an avatar said.

Hocus-pocus! A secretary desk floated from the very air, landing on the stage. The desk dropped its front cover, revealing a dictating machine.

The Enchanter closed his eyes and dictated. "Trojan-proxy relay-server. Crash. %*#$+.@. Reboot. Punching-card bag. Update ready for upload. Bad file descriptor. Fetch file. Filling Workstation. Operation now in progress. System reload. Ching, ping, ping, piggy bank, oink. File backup. The mind the question and arrows of time. The calamity of so long a life."

I jumped from my seat, leaping onto the stage. I grabbed his swinging head, slapping my hand over his mouth. "Speak English! I don't know the meaning of half that gibberish and I don't believe you do either!"

Everyone gasped.

The Enchanter had put my face on a milk carton, but there was no recognition in his eyes. He must be running low on memory due to the virus infecting him.

Quick, I ran back to my chair.

"Abracadabra then," the Enchanter said in a bored voice. His chains fell and his straitjacket unraveled. The Enchanter landed on his feet, bowing to the audience, who gave him a standing ovation.

One cyber being clapped his hands too slowly, and the Enchanter vaporized him with a zap of his fingers.

"I suppose you want a hat trick." The Enchanter pulled his top hat from his head. He circled a wand around the inside, displaying its empty contents.

The Enchanter yanked March-Hare from his hat, holding the hare by its long floppy ears.

March-Hare was still mad and had obviously been in a brawl. One front tooth was broken and his eye blackened. The bunny wore boxing gloves and kept trying to swing at me.

The Enchanter pulled a measuring tape from his top hat, measuring March-Hare. "You are as short as May, but longer than February. A jacket will do," he said, snapping his fingers.

He transformed the mad March-Hare into a furry strait jacket. The Enchanter dropped March-Hare back in his hat, which he then placed snugly on his head. The hat jiggled, the hare trying to escape strait jacket.

The Enchanter waved his hand, vanishing in a puff of smoke.

He reappeared on a giant, super-chip, suspended above the audience. The Enchanter had changed to sorcerer's robes. His wand was now a light pen, which he zapped across the audience.

The Enchanter held up his wand, and the crowd gasped. "Am I not your Central Processing Unit? I *am* the CPU I *am* the computer and order thousands of instructions a second. With a blink, I am here. I am there. I am everywhere. Yet, I cannot find the Gnome King. That little twerp invited a virus in. Who knows where the Gnome King is?" he thundered.

All the cyber beings quaked in their seats.

The Enchanter squeezed his fists, screaming, "I am going to start executing each of you, until someone squeals. Off with your heads! You, the disk doctor." He pointed his light pent to a man in a white suit, carrying a doctor's bag.

The man froze, his eyeballs spinning like two disks.

Grim Reaper swept the doctor up in her long arms. She threw the screeching doctor into a spinning pit surrounded by red bricks. Everyone cringed at his screams.

"I'm coming through. Make way," an important-sounding voice sang out.

"It's the Garbage-Collector," said a hushed voice. "The Collector burns up all the used memory, and recycles the ashes. Thank goodness, he has shown up to distract the Enchanter; otherwise, our CPU might delete us all. The virus has maddened the Enchanter. It is lunacy to delete the disk doctor during a plague. If the disks break, the computer can't function."

A fire-breathing dragon flapped his wings before the Enchanter.

The crowd gasped. "The Collector is pale and is, also, infected," a few voices murmured.

"What have you for us, Draggy," the Enchanter said, stroking the dragon's cheek.

"I know who the villain is who let in the virus to destroy Computer Land. The virus was carried in the belly of a Trojan horse."

I pulled my scarf up to the top of my head.

22. A Brother for a Brother

The crowd cheered at the dragon called the Collector.

I smacked at its claws.

My doppelganger suddenly appeared, pushing me from the chair. "I'm with the Gnome King," the other Alicia sang.

The Collector grabbed my shoulders, dragging me to the Enchanter.

The Enchanter formed his eyebrows like thunderbolts, causing an explosion.

Alakazam! A guillotine fell on the stage, the sharp blade coming down with a bang.

The Enchanter glared down at me from his floating super-chip. He zapped me.

I landed at the Enchanter's feet in an ungraceful heap. The mirrored surface was slippery.

The cyber beings wondered about me. "The creature isn't an avatar," one said.

"Yet, it looks like a flat avatar" another said.

"The creature appears more like a photograph," someone else said.

"A GIF file, perhaps?" one asked.

"You mean, a picture come to life, like an animated GIF?" another added.

"Yes, that's it. The creature is flat and two-dimensional, like a moving picture, an animated GIF."

The Enchanter walked with his hands grasped behind his back. "You're a malicious user," he hissed at me.

"It's a user!" All the cyber beings chattered, pointing at me.

"A user has never been inside the *Arena of Memory Chips* before," they said excitedly.

They all stood on their seats, peering at me.

"The user has legs," they exclaimed.

"The user's brain is weak, though," someone noted.

"No wonder users need us to solve their problems and entertain them." They all clapped with their own self-importance.

The Enchanter tugged my hair so I had to roll my eyes up to look at him.

"I had an accident and fell off a Trojan horse. I did not know he swallowed a computer virus. Anyway, the virus is just a bunch of fleas, eating everything in their path. Don't you have any flea collars or Slime-Vanish?" I said.

The Enchanter turned all shades of red. "Does this look like a pet store, you imbecile? No shopping mall is here. This is not the Internet. I'm surprised an imbecile user like you is the virus leader."

The Enchanter pointed his light pen at me.

I fell to my knees, covering my face with my hands.

"I suppose you must have a proper trial." The Enchanter motioned to a server. "Download trial software from the Internet."

A desk emerged and landed in front of the Enchanter. A judge's gavel loomed in his hand.

Ten judges marched across the super-chip. They sat behind the Enchanter with dirty, bare feet, showing beneath their robes. They wore wigs like English judges. They sat on the stifling air, because the Enchanter did not offer them chairs.

"We must hurry. The Trial Software expires in five minutes, because justice was never really purchased," the Enchanter said, smiling slyly.

"Don't I even get a lawyer?"

"You are a trial, User," the Enchanter said, rolling his eyes. "You should have stayed on your side of the monitor."

"I wish I had," I said and swallowed the lump in my throat.

"Oh, very well, you may have a lawyer," the Enchanter said. He blew a whistle.

Stinky strolled onto the super chip. The computer bug carried a jar containing the head of Logic.

Illogic walked behind Stinky. His head was still twisted on his shoulders, so his face tried to run backward. Illogic fumbled and stumbled across the super-chip. He was dressed in a black robe, and his pipe stuck out from a long, white wig that fell in ringlets to his back. He carried a briefcase.

The Enchanter rubbed his hands together and laughed. "I have just downloaded a law degree from the Internet, a plug-in to Illogic's program. Say hello to your lawyer, User. Illogic will defend you for killing his brother with the virus you released into our world."

"But that's so unfair," Axel yelled.

"What fragment are you from, that you dare to question me, Ghost?" the Enchanter said.

"I am a fragment of her brother's doppelganger."

"Come down here then." The Enchanter pointed his wand at Axel and levitated him to the superchip.

I ran to the ghostly Axel and he tried to hug me.

"An eye-for-an-eye is fair, is it not, Brother?" the Enchanter said to Axel. The Enchanter smiled at me. "And you didn't think we had religion here, did you, User?"

"You have a Bible in the archives," I said.

The Enchanter had a gleam in his eyes. "Defend the user," he said to Illogic."

Mumblings erupted from Illogic, like the village idiot. He talked to himself, with his head facing east. He responded with his head facing west. He asked questions with his head looking up to the North. He answered his questions looking down to the South. He flung his hands in the air in argument with himself.

"Enough! The trial software has expired," the Enchanter said.

Slowly, the judges vanished.

23. Ever Been Vomited by a Trash Can?

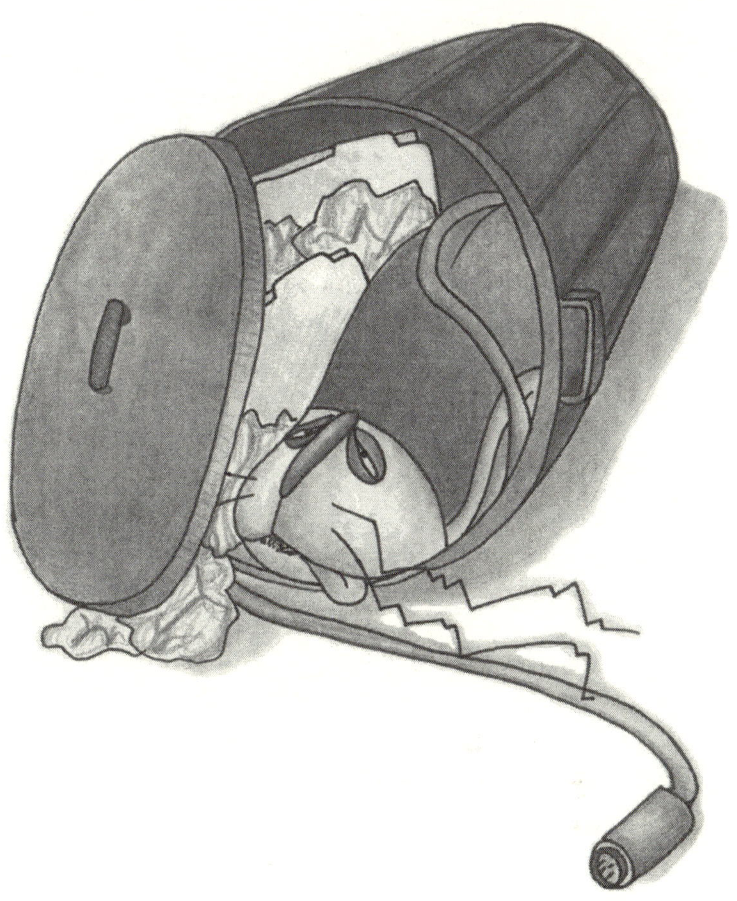

"Bring in the recycle bin, Draggy," the Enchanter said to the dragon.

A trash can appeared.

"Now the witness for your next trial, Alicia." The Enchanter pointed his light pen at the recycle bin. "Open sesame!"

The lid popped open, revealing Louse-the-Mouse sleeping in the trash. "Wake up, you idiot wheelman!"

Louse's blue tongue hung out, and his dazed eyes opened. "Louse must find his center, center," the mouse said repeatedly. He shook his head and crawled from the bin.

I was not the only one happy the mouse was salvaged. Axel moved his mouth to my ear and whispered. "Your brother has the mouse back. Perhaps Axel can find a way to get you out of here."

"What have you to do with the user Alicia?" the Enchanter asked Louse.

"Don't remember, Governor," Louse said.

"Then I shall have to remember for you," the Enchanter said. He shot lasers from his eyes, hypnotizing Louse and me.

The Enchanter released us, and we spun in circles.

"The hacker, Dormouse, hacked Louse and gave Alicia access to our system files," the Enchanter, howled, turning purple.

The Enchanter disappeared in a cloud of smoke. He materialized standing on his head. "You make us inefficient, Alicia! I save the rodent from the recycle bin and because of you, must permanently delete him. Fraggy, purge the mouse."

Grim Reaper picked up the sobbing Louse and carried him over to Fraggy, who resembled a giant green dumpster on legs.

Fraggy opened his huge metal mouth that had jagged, teeth-like edges.

Grim Reaper threw Louse in.

The metal mouth slammed shut.

The audience cringed at the muffled squeaks between the grinding of metal teeth.

The Enchanter floated above me, smiling. "The disk-defragger, Fraggy, will sweep clean the address attached to your brother, so other programs can move into his space. In other words, Axel is not to be recycled."

"Don't worry about me, Alicia," Axel whispered, "I'm just a ghost. You must not endanger yourself more. You may still have a chance to escape. I overheard the cyber beings talking about a portal."

"I'm so sorry, Axel," I said, sobbing.

"Listen carefully to the mouse's suffering. In this same manner, every trace of your brother's existence will be wiped out, as though he never was," the Enchanter said.

"No!" I dropped to my knees, begging.

Axel hung his ghostly head in defeat. He placed a hand on my shoulder. "Don't feel bad, Alicia. I'm just a fragment, after all."

The Enchanter lifted his hands to the cyber creatures, who sat captivated by the entertainment. "Hear me all. My sentence is that the hacker Alicia be deleted forever." The Enchanter pounded his gavel and turned his thumb down.

The audience cheered.

"You can't exterminate Alicia. Her technology is mine," a voice cackled with glee.

It was the witch, riding a broom and waving her patent documents.

"No scrap of paper commands me! Off with your head!" the Enchanter shouted. He pointed his light pen at the witch, zapping her.

The witch fell off her broom. Her head rolled into the pit.

The Enchanter must have memory problems. He forgot about his threat to execute Axel first. "Off with your head," he said, aiming his light pen at me.

"Run, Alicia," Axel yelled.

Grim Reaper grabbed me.

The Gnome King suddenly appeared. He spoke through a bullhorn. "Enchanter, zap me into a desktop icon. I shall stop the virus and spare your life."

"You shall spare my life? Midget!" the Enchanter roared.

"Do not call me a midget!" The Gnome King stomped like a two-year-old having a temper tantrum. "Make me an icon, or I'll take the virus to the Internet and infect the entire world. Everyone will blame your computer, Enchanter."

The super-chip glowed green, and a yellow light surrounded the Enchanter. "Do not dare to blackmail me," the Enchanter roared.

24. I Broke Some Links

The Enchanter turned the Gnome King into a stone garden statue.

The Enchanter sniffled as if he had a cold. "We are running low on power due to the virus." He sneezed.

"Quiet!" he yelled at the gasping crowd. "And stop your infernal nagging, hag!" The Enchanter referred to the witch whose hand refused to let go of my patent. Her head was still talking, demanding that the Enchanter release me into her custody.

The Enchanter blew a fart, shutting the witch up with magic gas.

"Backup," Axel said in a panicky voice.

"Never!" the Enchanter growled.

I pointed to the fleas flying over the darkening sky. "Backup," I screeched.

The Enchanter rapped Illogic on his head. "Nitwit, why didn't you remember the *backup* file? We can save ourselves, by restoring to a point in time before the virus struck. Send for the file clerk, Sir Broken-Links."

Everyone danced on their seats, while Illogic ran backwards to fetch the file clerk.

I did cartwheels.

Axel spun on one finger.

Neat! The *backup* file would restore the computer to before the virus struck. Maybe we would go back in time to a period before the gnomes kidnapped me.

A crystal ball rolled across the super-chip. The ball glowed, revealing the image of file cabinets. Drawers slid open and files flipped open. The crystal ball put on reading glasses, scanning documents in the files.

A white mist swirled around the glass ball, lips forming in the mist. "Some files are missing from the *backup* and *recovery* folders, my master."

"What files, Sir Broken-Links?" the Enchanter said, his eyes icing.

"The *boot* file," the crystal ball said in a loud, whispery voice.

"But how will we restart? Being without a *boot* file is like trying to start a car without a key," the Enchanter said.

"Other files have vanished. My prediction is that the backup and recovery process is too unstable. If you proceed on this dangerous path, we may be shut down, forever," the ball added in an ominous tone.

A hush filled the arena.

Grim Reaper approached the crystal ball with a hammer held over her head.

The ball glowed red. "Do not shatter me. I am not responsible for this mess! The last time I rolled down the backup tree, all was in order. Someone has broken vital directory branches and thrown files away."

"I shall conduct a séance to discover what happened to the missing files," the Enchanter said.

A table dropped in front of the Enchanter, along with three zombies seated around the table. The zombies were computer forensic tools used to dig up files involving computer crimes.

The Enchanter sat in the fourth chair beside the zombies. A spotlight shone on the Enchanter, and he went into a trance. "I am channeling the spirit of Ada Lovelace, the woman who wrote the first computer program in 1842, for the Babbage Analytical Engine. My dear Ada, are you there?"

"I'm here, Enchanter," a sweet voice said in a British accent.

"Show us what happened to the *boot* file. Can you do that, Honey Bunches?"

"Oh, Axel, I did a bad thing in the file room," I whispered.

Axel groaned.

The spotlight shone on my head. Ghostly images played in the background of me in the file room.

"You are to suffer the fate that was to be Sir Broken-Links. I will shatter you, User. First, you must watch your brother die," the Enchanter thundered.

Just then, the stinging fleas attacked with vengeance.

The virus weakened the Enchanter. His servers helped him to rise. "I have such a headache. My memory leaks," the Enchanter moaned, stumbling on his robe.

Everyone screamed and ran for their lives from the *Arena of Memory Chips*.

I stumbled behind Axel.

Fraggy, the disk-defragger, chased us with its stomach open like a garbage dumpster.

I slipped and shook my foot, trying to dislodge whatever held onto me. It clawed at my leg.

Fraggy twisted and spun, inching its jaws closer.

Suddenly, I was snatched by the neck and sucked up like a vacuum.

Whatever it was carried me upward.

Fraggy snapped its jaws at me.

Chills crawled up my spine at the steaming computer, filling with fog and smoke.

There was a jolt, followed by an eerie stillness.

Eke! The virus deleted me! I could not see my hand in front of my face.

There was another jerk.

Whoosh!

I rode on a lightning-fast ride.

Whatever was happening to me was both scary and exciting at the same time. It felt like I was whirling through a tunnel at the speed of light. I kept rubbing my body and patting my head to make sure the virus was not deleting me.

25. I Ride on a Personal Data Transporter

Flash! I was back in the study, hanging onto a USB thumb drive.

Axel grinned down at me. "Using the ghostly fragment of my doppelganger, I was able to pull you back with my *personal data transport*," my brother said.

Oddly, I do not remember the USB Flash Drive being bigger than my hand.

"Good thing I clicked on the Safely-Remove-Hardware icon, else you might not have made it in one piece," he said.

Yes, I was safe, but..."One piece? I am the size of the monitor screen. It's not funny!" I yelled at Axel.

My giant brother picked me up by the armpits as he would a doll. "Geez, you're flat, Alicia. No wonder you could hitch a ride on the flash-drive," he said, chuckling. "But I wonder you're not smaller than the thumb drive. Somehow you grew a bit."

I tried to punch him and kick him.

Axel swung me around making me dizzy.

"Let me go, you creep!" I shouted.

"That's the thanks I get for saving you, little sister? Geez, you look funny. Our Beagle is bigger than you are."

I kicked him.

"Your shoe tickles," he said, laughing.

"Let me down," I screeched. I grabbed onto his nostril and bit down hard.

"Ouch! That stings. Okay, there." Axel set me gently down on the rug and then kneeled so he would not have to stoop to my shortness.

"How am I supposed to grow? Look at me! I'm like a foot tall."

I heard giggling.

"Quit laughing," I yelled.

"I'm not," Axel said.

I still heard giggling. "Shut up," I hollered.

"You shut up!" Axel said.

"I told you to stop laughing at me."

"I'm not!"

The vomit-green carpet was like ankle-deep grass. "Figure out how to maximize my size!"

"Only if you stop acting mean."

"You owe me, Alicia, and not just for sending a USB Flash Drive to get you out. I covered for you. Between trying to help you and telling Mom I gave you permission to spend the night at your friend's house, I got in trouble. Mom hit the roof, ordering me to clear it with her or Dad next time."

"We need to get our stories straight. What friend did I stay with?"

"Sally, that phreak, the only real friend you have."

"Sally gave up phreaking, because her mom gave her a cell phone with free long distance service, so she doesn't have to hack into phone systems anymore. Instead, Sally hacks into computers now. I swear my days of hacking are over after this adventure." Communication with the shadowy, ghostly Axel had been so much easier. "Well, thanks for all your help," I mumbled, regretting every mean trick I ever played on Axel.

The door lay on the study floor. Dickens, our black and white kitty, ran into the room.

His fur stood on end. Dickens crouched low and hissed.

I screamed, and grew a bit.

Dickens reached out its claws, and I shrieked, growing bigger.

The cat opened its mouth and I wailed, growing another inch.

"That's it, Alicia. Breathe deeply. I forgot oxygen regulates human cell growth. The fresh air probably made you grow the size of the monitor," Axel said. He grabbed a science book from the bookcase and started fluttering the pages.

I bawled and hollered, taking in gobs of oxygen, to fuel my temper. I wanted to box Axel's ears. It was just like my brother, to be more interested in science than the fact that Dickens was trying to put me in his mouth. Our cat's teeth kept sliding off my paper-thin body.

Yuck! Dickens slobbered spoiled-tuna saliva all over me. I smelled like dead fish.

At last, I grew to my normal height and growled at the cat.

Dickens ran from the room with his tail between his legs.

I was exhausted with growing pains. Cat slobber stuck to my hair. So many things were broken in the study. The mirror was…

"Eek! I am normal-sized but a flat freak! I can't go to school, ever again!"

"Breathe, Alicia, breathe," Axel said.

I did as instructed and ended up over breathing. I hyperventilated which felt as if I could not breathe. I was breathing too fast and felt dizzy. My eyes spun in circles, the study twirling.

Poof! I inflated, mushroomed, and fattened. "Eek! I'm going to blow up like a balloon!" I lay on the carpet, like a fat beetle on its back unable to even roll over.

"Alicia, calm down. Push all the oxygen from your lungs, until your stomach touches your spine."

"That's it. Suck in your gut, as long as possible. Keep your mouth closed; expand your stomach, slowly."

I did as Axel instructed and sucked my stomach into the rug.

As I grew thinner, the study vibrated with screeches, sounding like a balloon deflating.

At last, I was back to my normal three-dimensional size.

Suddenly, there were two crashes in the room.

26. I'm Grounded for the Rest of my Life

Dad crashed into the room, nearly tripping on the door that was on the floor.

For no reason, the lamp fell from the bookcase about the same time Dad came into the room.

Dad stepped over me. He pointed at Axel, who was sitting at the desk with his hand on the game controller. "How many times must I tell you, Axel, that it's just a video game? You get so upset, if you lose. I just fixed that computer and you broke it. And you cracked the new monitor. When did you break the window?" Dad yelled, scowling at my brother.

"I broke the computer," I blurted out. "I'm to blame, Dad, for all the damage."

Dad stood over me with his fists on his hips. "You are going to pay for the broken lamp from your allowance, young lady."

I noticed a quick movement on the bookcase, followed by loud giggling.

Dad shook his finger in my face and shouted, "This is not funny, young lady."

I had not laughed but did not defend myself. I knew who shoved the lamp off the bookcase, and it was neither Axel nor me.

The top shelf of the bookcase belonged to Axel. Books about sailing, dog breeds, and dark fantasy novels filled his shelf.

The bottom bookshelf was mine. This shelf contained novels about witches, humorous cat stories, and classic books.

We shared the middle shelf. Computer pirating magazines leaned against my computer hacking magazines. At Axel's shelf end was a figure of an eye-patched pirate. At my end was a pony-tailed girl, waving a sword, hacking at a ceramic computer.

Something had grabbed onto my ankle right before I hitched a ride on the USB flash drive. March-Hare, my doppelganger the other Alicia, and a gnome had somehow hid in the Personal Data Transporter and escaped the computer through the USB port with me. However, they were all small.

March-Hare was the size of a bookend and pushed against the magazines. She was always a 3-D avatar so the spectacled bunny did not look odd. March-Hare pretended to be a white statue of a rabbit wearing a yellow polka dot bow. Aha! March-Hare blinked behind her computer glasses.

The gnome and the other Alicia were flat, just as I had been. My doppelganger was about the height of the monitor, so about 15 inches. The redheaded gnome was only about seven inches tall. They both stood on the same shelf as March-Hare. The other Alicia was at the right end, flat up against the wood, appearing like wallpaper on the bookcase shelf. The gnome did the same on the other end of the shelf.

Neither Dad nor Axel noticed anything odd about the bookcase.

March-Hare, the gnome, and my doppelganger all giggled again, in unison so it sounded like one loud laugh.

"You're still laughing?" Dad said to me.

"Yes," I quickly said, shifting my eyes to the snickering figures on the bookcase, and then back to my father.

Dad leaned closer to me. "Read my lips. You're grounded, Alicia."

I opened my mouth and laughed very loud in order to mask the laughter coming from the bookcase.

"What in tarnation happened to your braces?" Dad said.

"I sort of lost my braces."

"For the rest of your life, you are grounded. Do you hear me, miss?"

I nodded my head yes, of course, whatever you say, Dad. Sir. Sir Dad.

"Now clean up as much of this mess as you can," Dad said.

He patted Axel on the back. The two left the study, discussing me.

"You sister is incorrigible," Dad said.

"Ah, Alicia is not so bad, Dad," Axel said.

"But how can anyone lose their braces? How is that even possible?"

"With Alicia, anything is possible. My sister is a pro," Axel proudly said.

I tried to grab my doppelganger, but the other Alicia ran from the study. Are you aware that most hackers are not athletic? Cyber creatures are slippery little suckers. I spun and all three had vanished from the room.

Pictures dropped from the hall walls, crashing to the floor.

I looked down the hallway, littered with broken glass.

The other Alicia spun and grinned at me. She held the gnome's hand. The gnome was a bearded, ordinary-looking gnome. The gnome had already been in my bedroom and was dressed in fashion-doll clothes. I now regretted not throwing my last doll out. The gnome looked ridiculous, dressed in a loose, red, sequined dress. His cone hat tilted jauntily on his head, and his beard came to a point at his waist. He looked even sillier wobbling on yellow, plastic, high-heel sandals. The heels were tight, the straps bending his flat feet.

The gnome snarled at me and glared with beady eyes.

March-Hare hopped in front of them.

The bunny stopped hopping to take a poop on the hall rug.

My parents would blame Dickens for those pellets.

March-Hare then punched a hole in the wall and hopped sideways. She was still a crazy bunny.

I was about to run after the rascals when Dad yelled in a thundering voice, "Alicia, what did you break now?"

The three strolled down the hallway and into my parents' bedrooms. Gnomes love clothes. The beastie was probably going through Mom's dresser. Gnomes are good with a needle and thread. The gnome was probably making an outfit from mom's underwear.

Even more socks are going to vanish from the clothes dryer.

In the future, my family will blame me for mischief I really did not do.

"Alicia, I'm not going to tell you again to come down and eat your supper," Dad yelled.

"We're waiting for you," Mom shouted back.

"I'm coming!" I hollered.

I did not even have time to clean up. I shuffled on dirty, torn tennis shoes, towards the stairs.

With those three creatures making mischief in my house, I really am grounded for the rest of my life. Bummer!

Dictionary of Computer Words and Concepts

And a Taste of French, Voila!

Ada Lovelace

Ada, Countess of Loveless, was born in 1815. She is considered the first Computer programmer. Her love of math was scandalous for a female in the Nineteenth Century. Nevertheless, in 1842 and 1843, she bravely wrote an algorithm for processing Charles Babbage's analytical engine, the first mechanical, general-purpose computer. Ada's contribution went unrewarded until 1977, when the U.S. Department of Defense decided their weapon systems needed a gentler touch, so named their porky computer language after her.

address

Data, programs, and other softer in the computer are stored at an address on a hard drive so the CPU can find them.

aka

stands for *also known as*

algorithm

An algorithm is a solution to a problem, written as steps and paths. For example, if homework vanished, an algorithm might first check if the dog ate it, followed by the next step of checking if the computer deleted it, followed by a step to remember if the homework was ever actually done, followed by a written excuse by a parent. Various paths of panic could branch out from each step.

animated GIF

an image file that, when executed, is not static but animated—such as a television cartoon versus the static poster of a character from the cartoon

antivirus

software written to avoid or sniff out and destroy computer viruses

appliance-gnomes

Appliance-gnomes are pudgy and poorly dressed. They live in plumbing with rats. They slide down laundry pipes and dive into washing machines or dryers. They love to steal a sock to wear on their heads for warmth. When hungry, they invade microwave ovens, refrigerators, and freezers.

au revoir

goodbye in French

avatar

An avatar represents the user in the computer. An example is a figure acting as the user in a video game.

background

an image always displayed on the desktop, beneath icons and executing programs

backup

files saved on external storage

barebones security

a risky, minimum-security program, which is supposed to protect a computer from viruses, data theft, and other threats

beasties
: See computer-gnomes.

block
: a chunk of a computer program

boot file
: The boot file kicks the computer awake.

breadcrumbs
: Some web pages leave breadcrumbs, which is a path of web pages clicked to get to the current webpage. A user can backtrack and easily return to the other pages.

Brute Force Blocking Software
: software used to block brute force attempts at gaining access to a computer

bug
: an error that causes a program to either crash or give incorrect results

buggy
: an unstable system with a computer bug or bugs

byte
: Programmers write computer programs (software) in computer languages. A compiler in the computer converts the programs to bytes, a byte being a *0* or a *1*. These bytes are machine language. A computer can only understand patterns of these two digits, *zero* meaning off and *one* meaning on. The computer reads the digits as a series of *off* and *on* lights. A computer is fast because it processes the flashes of light so rapidly in a computer chip, it is undetectable to the human eye.

C drive

Drives are used for computer storage and are identified by letters. The C drive is normally reserved for the main hard disk drive.

camera

Some computers have a tiny camera or lens, normally mounted at the top of a laptop or monitor. Images are automatically sent in digital form to the computer. Video software is used to control the camera.

Cheri

French for *precious* or *darling*

circuit board

a thin board, consisting of printed circuits and inserted into a computer's hardware slots to add features

computer

A computer is a bossy machine with a big ego that thinks it knows everything. Some think a computer is magic.

computer beasties

see computer-gnomes

computer bug

see bug

computer engineer

an engineer who develops computer systems

computer-gnomes

These gnomes are dangerous cousins of garden-gnomes, appliance-gnomes, and pencil-gnomes. Computer-gnomes are highly intelligent and infamously bratty. These rascals delete files, randomly freeze computers, and engage in all manner of high-tech hijinks. The gnomes sing in harmony, as they mine the hardware with tiny hammers, and pull wires with their pointy teeth. Their voices sound like a whirling fan, and a wobbling DVD or CD.

computer language
: a language used to write computer programs (software)

computer virus
: a malicious program, usually meant to destroy software in a computer, or steal data

computer hacking
: breaking into another person's computer, as a challenge, to snoop, or for malicious reasons

computer-icon
: an image on the desktop, which represents a data file, command, or program

computer illiterate
: a person who is afraid to use a computer, or has no computer skills

computer program
: see software

computer pirating
: downloading and sharing copyrighted media, without the creator's permission

computer security
: software that protects a computer from hackers, crackers, and malicious programs

CPU

CPU stands for Central Processing Unit. The CPU is the brains of the computer. Without the CPU, nothing can happen.

cracker

a criminal who breaks into computers to steal for profit or destruction

crash

when a program exits without completing its task, or freezes

croissant

a crescent-shaped flaky roll

cyber

relating to the world of computers

D drive

This is a drive used for computer storage and identified by a letter. The D drive is sometimes reserved for recovery.

data byte

A data byte is one character of data. For example, the letter H or the character ~ is a data byte.

degauss

removes discoloration from a monitor

delete with wiping

delete a file from the computer, so that it cannot be restored from the recycle bin or trash can

desktop
: a graphical user interface with clickable icons, menus, and background wallpaper

directory
: A directory contains files. A directory can contain other directories. A directory is a way to organize data.

download
: transferring a file from the Internet to a PC, laptop, tablet, cell phone, etc.

DVD
: a digital video disk

DVD drive
: hardware that can play a DVD

E drive
: Drives used for computer storage are identified by letters.

egghead
: one who is very smart and loves math, science and other nerdy subjects

electronic
: a device that runs with electricity and has tiny electrical parts such as microchips

en garde
: French for *on your guard*

ergonomic mouse
: a mouse designed so that it prevents repetitive motion injuries

familiar

This is an animal (usually a cat) used by a witch for spying. The familiar has the ability to speak to the witch.

file

A computer reads and writes digital files, or documents.

firewall

computer security, which prevents unwanted access through a computer's network

forensic tools

software used to examine digital data when a computer crime is believed to have taken place

fragment

part of a computer file that has become separated from the file

French mousse

a pudding-like desert

garden-gnomes

These gnomes are shy farmers who eat dirt, hide behind flowers and blades of grass. They are sometimes spotted at airports trying to hop into luggage. Their dream is to landscape a foreign country.

GIF file

a type of image file with a *.gif* extension to its name

graphical user interface

This type of interface allows a user to interact with a computer, using a mouse. This makes the experience more pleasant because of images on the screen, rather than just text. This is also called a GUI.

GUI

see graphical user interface

hacker

Hackers are not malicious, like crackers. A hacker hacks away at the keyboard to break into a computer. Hackers are mainly curious about how things work or like a challenge.

handle

a nickname that a hacker, cracker, or computer pirate goes by

hard disk drive

see hard drive

hard drive

a storage device of a computer that is a piece of hardware

hardware

Hardware is the physical parts that make up a computer system, such as the monitor, keyboard, etc. Hardware is, also, inside the computer case, such as the electronics.

help menu

a menu that provides help for the user

high-tech

highly advanced technology

icon

an image that represents a program, command, or file

Internet

The Internet is a super network, which connects computers and other networks across the world. The Internet is also called the World Wide Web, the WWW, or the Web.

Java

a computer language

Java Virtual Machine (JVM)

software that runs Java programs

keyboard

hardware or software with a mixed-up alphabet that the user types on to communicate with a computer or tablet

mademoiselle

French for *my young lady*

Ma Petite

French for *my child*

memory

Software in a computer can only execute in memory. Thus, a computer program is transferred to memory before being executed.

memory banks

This is the computer memory and is usually spread out in memory chips.

memory chips

Memory chips are little pieces of powerful hardware that contain the computer's memory. Programs and data are stored in memory during execution for quick retrieval.

millisecond

Because computers are so fast, time is measured in milliseconds. One second is 1,000 milliseconds. For instance, the blink of an eye is about 300 milliseconds, or ¼ of a second. Very fast computers operate in microseconds, which is a millionth of a second. Supercomputers can operate in nanoseconds, which is a billionth of a second.

monitor

a computer's display

monitor's guts

hardware: the wires, bolts, screws, chips, inside the hard case of the monitor

monitor screen

the part of the monitor that shows the images, like a TV screen

monochrome

in black, white, and gray, with no bright color

Monsieur

French for *Mister*

motherboard

the main, printed circuit board that contains the computer's most important electronics

mouse
: a pointing device, which allows a user to click on items displayed on a monitor

mouse clicker
: buttons on a mouse, which are pressed to request an action from the computer

mouse pad
: This is a rubbery-type pad, usually cluttered by dust and the droppings of a user's hand. The mouse pad is an apartment where the computer mouse hangs out.

multi-user edition
: an edition of a computer game, which allows the game to be played by more than one player

network
: This is a group of connected computers. For example, the World Wide Web is a network of computers.

oxymoron
: a phrase containing words with opposite meaning, such as "liquid gas" or "awfully pretty"

password
: a secret word or character string, requested at login, which allows access to a computer protected by the password

PC
: personal computer such as a desktop computer, laptop, or tablet

pencil-gnomes
: They eat lead.

personal data transport

This is a thumb-sized piece of hardware used to store files or transfer files from one computer to another. They are sometimes called USB flash drives or thumb drives.

phreaking

The word phreak comes from the words phone and freak. It is the act of breaking into telephone networks.

piggy-backer

a user who gains free access to the Internet by using someone else's Internet service, without him or her knowing about it

pirate-gnomes

These sneaky, mercenary sailors enjoy thievery and pillaging in sinks, bathtubs, showers, and swimming pools. Pirate-gnomes are good swimmers. They, also, pirate in computers, selling their booty on the black market PirateTreasureBay.

PirateTreasureBay

a virtual flea market, where pirates unload their junk on hyper-shoppers and shopping addicts

plug-in

This program adds features to another program. For example, a web browser, which is a program, might use a plug-in to play a movie on a user's computer.

printed circuit board

a thin board, inserted into the computer, which connects and supports electronic parts program

A computer program consists of a task or tasks carried out by a computer. A program is, also, software. An example is a calculator program, which adds, subtracts, etc.

program crash

This is a premature ending of a program. The program vanishes from the screen, gives an unrecoverable error, or freezes up, becoming unresponsive to all mouse clicks.

programmer

a person who writes computer programs

programming code

A computer program is made up of programming code. The code, or program, is written in a programming language. A computer program and programming code is the same thing.

programming language

a language used to write computer programs

punching-card

In the days of dinosaur computers that were the size of a house, a computer read the holes of punch cards. There was no mouse and no personal computers. Only businesses used computers in those old-fashioned days.

quiche

a French dish resembling an egg pie

RAT

A RAT, which stands for Remote Administration Tool, is software that allows someone to remotely control a computer or a device on the computer.

RATs are sometimes used to fix a computer remotely. RATS can be used for malicious reasons to take control of a computer without permission.

reboot

restarting the computer from scratch

recovery file

a file necessary for recovering a sick computer by restoring it back in time before the computer got sick

refresh

a monitor redrawing its images on the screen

screen

the visual portion of a monitor

screen burn-in

When a non-moving image is left in place for too long on a monitor without refreshing, the image will burn into the screen as a ghostly image. Screen burn-in is usually permanent unless repaired by special software. A screen saver can be used to prevent a background image from becoming screen burn-in when the computer is left on for a long period of time without any action from a user, such as typing on the keyboard or using the mouse.

security hole

a weakness in computer security

shareware

free software that can be downloaded from the Internet

shut down

Clicking on the *shut down* command, causes the computer to exit all programs before turning off.

software

This is computer code written in a computer language. Software, program, and code are different words for the same thing. Hardware is the muscle and software is the brains of the computer. For example, a computer game is software. (see program)

soufflé

a fluffy French dish made from egg yolks, stiff egg whites, and cheese, fruit or fish

spaghetti code

parts of a computer program written with so many twists, turns, and branches, making the software difficult for a programmer to figure out the code and make changes or fix errors

spam

unwanted email, usually advertisements sent to thousands or millions of people

spell checker

This smarty-pants program checks the spelling of a user. A spell checker sometimes cannot tell if a word is used correctly in a sentence. For example, *I no your name* might pass a spell checker.

spyware

software sneakily installed by the Internet on a user's computer, which typically sends back data about the user's web surfing habits surf

to browse the World Wide Web

surge protector

This is an electrical strip, or special outlet, used for machines like computers or televisions. A surge protector shields equipment plugged into it from damage created by surges of electricity, such as lightning causes.

system file

a file or program used exclusively by the CPU for starting up, shutting down, or managing the computer

technology

Technology is advanced scientific knowledge useful to the public or industry. An example is smart machines such as computers, tablets, or smart phones.

trial software

a program downloaded free that expires if not purchased by a certain date

Trojan

a computer virus, which pretends to be useful, but is actually malicious

Trojan horse

see Trojan

Trojan-gnomes

an offshoot of the appliance-gnome; a sneaky, mercenary gnome, who enjoys fighting and breaking things

Trojan-virus
: see Trojan

update
: installing a new version of software

upload
: copying a file to a user's computer from the Internet, USB flash drive, CD or some other device

UPS
: UPS stands for Uninterruptible Power Supply. An UPS is heavy and resembles a big box because it has powerful batteries. The UPS provides power to a computer in case the electricity goes out. UPS are useful for hospitals and other places where it is important to keep the computer running during a power outage.

USB connector
: This is a connector on a computer for USB devices to be connected. A USB device could be a mouse, keyboard, or flash drive.

USB flash drive
: see USB transporter

USB thumb drive
: see USB transporter

USB transporter
: This is a personal data transport, also known as flash drive or thumb drive. A USB storage device flashes as it transports data to a computer. It fits in your pocket.

version two

This is the second release of software with fixed bugs and usually, added features. A new version of software sometimes introduces new bugs.

video game

a visual, electronic game, played with a graphical user interface

virtual

This is an imitation, created by a computer. For instance, a virtual dog is not a real dog, but behaves as if it is a dog.

virtual reality

This is a world created by a computer. The cyber world seems real due to the human senses experiencing virtual sight, taste, touch, sound, smell, etc. Virtual reality equipment immerses the user in the virtual world so that the experience seems real.

virus

This is malicious software usually hidden in a trusted program. Infected programs copy the virus to other programs.

voila

French for, *see there*!

user manual

a computer help manual

wallpaper

a pattern or picture always visible in a monitor's background

WAR file

WAR stands for Web application ARchive. This collection of Java files make up a web application. For instance, a web file might be one email. A web application would be the mail program that allows a user to read, write, forward, reply to mail, etc.

web

see Internet

World Wide Web (WWW)

see Internet

worm

a malicious computer program used as a hacking tool to detect vulnerabilities in the operating system of a computer

worm-flu

This is malicious software. Worm-flu uses a network to send copies of itself to other computers on the network. The worm does not need to be hidden in a program, as a virus does.

List of Illustrations

Please note that all composite digital pictures in this book were created by Belinda Vasquez Garcia. Most of the images in *Alicia's Misadventures in Computer* Land are meant to reflect the world of the computer such as background wallpapers, and avatars.

About the Stupendous Author

Belinda Vasquez Garcia is a native of California. She has also lived in New Mexico, Texas, Arizona, Colorado, and Florida.

Before writing full time, she worked as a Computer Programmer, Software Engineer, Java Applications Programmer, and Web Developer. She earned a Bachelor's degree in Applied Mathematics from the University of New Mexico.

Belinda has won eleven awards for her numerous books, including:

- five Fantasy Awards
- two Historical Fiction Awards
- one Audio Book Award
- one eBook Award
- one Multi-cultural Fiction Award
- one Books into Movies Award

She lives with her husband Bob, dog Toby, and cat Shakespeare.

Lastly, Belinda would like to thank you for purchasing *Alicia's Misadventures in Computer Land.*

website: http://magicprose.com/chaos-computing/

19702345R00115

Made in the USA
Middletown, DE
30 April 2015